ENTANGLEMENTS

Assa Raymond Baker

GOOD 2 GO PUBLISHING

ENTANGLEMENTS
Written by Assa Raymond Baker
Cover Design: Davida Baldwin, Odd Ball Designs
Typesetter: Mychea
ISBN: 978-1-947340-78-7
Copyright © 2022 Good2Go Publishing
Published 2022 by Good2Go Publishing
7311 W. Glass Lane • Laveen, AZ 85339
www.good2gopublishing.com
https://twitter.com/good2gobooks
G2G@good2gopublishing.com
www.facebook.com/good2gopublishing
www.instagram.com/good2gopublishing

Acknowledgments

First and always, I give up praise to my Lord God Most High. If I was without God's light, I would simply be another member of the walking dead.

After getting over the shock of all of this time that I'm currently serving, I decided to become a full-time storyteller. I really love telling stories, and it feels amazing to see them in print. There's only one name on this on this cover: mine. I want my name when seen by my readers to spark excitement, knowing that when they spend their hard-earned dollars and sit down to invest their time, it'll be well spent.

But keeping it ten thousand, it takes far more than me to take what's banging around in my hard head and put it into the readers' hands. For that, I must give immediate thanks to my publisher and the entire G2G publishing team for all of their hard work and patience. Thanks, everyone!

I was asked once why don't I write a full-length book. To be honest, I don't know what that is. I tell the story that's in my head until it's out. My novels are hot, shocking, sexy, fast-paced page-turners, written to give the readers the fix they need. There's a strict kinda discipline required to write the way I do. I give you just enough background information about my characters and the locations to spark the imagination, and I run on from there. Trust me, writing the way I do makes it way hard to meet my publisher's required word count, so for you who don't like my style of storytelling, thank you for your investment, and I'm always looking forward to reading what you have to say about my craft.

Now I must send a tremendous thanks to the following people: Rhonda, my muse and partner. You're my first adviser in my writings and in life. To Didi, my lost love. To my beautiful mother and stepmom for your love. To my sisters and brothers for their love. Hell, to my entire family for their love and support and all they do to keep me straight in the mind while I'm wandering through this madhouse. Lastly, thanks to all my thugs and thugettes locked down in these cold BOP & DOC cells. We share the same struggles. It gets hard and heavy, but we keep on moving like it's easy because we're stronger than most. Much love and may all be well!

Assa Out!

Forward

Tone's custom candy-painted, ruby-red, gold-trimmed 1989 Chevy SS Impala pushed 50 mph, doing over 20 miles over the posted speed limit as it raced across the Twenty-Seventh Street Bridge. Tilt, the fancy car's driver, immediately lowered the volume of Lil Boosie & Webbie's song, "Do It Stick." They were pounding out of the two powerful Sony subwoofers in the trunk of his car as he slowed and stopped at the stoplight at the end of the bridge. Any other time, at the speed he was traveling, the thug would've blown right through the stoplight, but it just so happened to be a police car preparing to make a turn east off of Twenty-Seventh Street when he got there. The young thug kept his eye on the patrol car as it made its turn. He used the time to break down and roll up a blunt for them to blow on their way to pick up the car they had paid one of the youngsters steal for them and park behind an abandoned house on Twenty-Second and Scott earlier that evening.

"Folks, let me burn that nigga G? Fuck him!" Tone exclaimed as they turned onto Scott Street and parked. "I never liked his fool ass, straight up. He be always trying to down talk me an shit, like he better than a muthafucka or some shit," Tone said as they got out of the car and commenced walking through the alley toward the other car.

"You just don't like him because he use to pimp on your mama," Tilt teased, getting behind the wheel of the stolen forest-green 2002 Grand Prix. As soon as he was seated, he drew his gun and placed it under his right thigh for easy access.

"Correction, I don't like him because he use to beat on my mama," Tone retorted, taking his place beside him and pulling on a pair of black workmen's gloves.

"Aye, G, don't fuck up this hit, fam, 'cause we won't get another chance this sweet at that nigga out in the open," he warned him.

"Sweet or not, the nigga a bitch, and I'm on dat! But on the G, I won't miss his fat ass," Tone swore while simultaneously checking the ammo inside two extended chips that he'd brought with him for his modified Glock 27.

"Yeah, he all that, but he's known to keep a few shooters on his team. Fam, don't forget that when there's money behind a nigga there's always a fool or two that will do whatever for him just to say that they did it. Remember that," Title told his younger partner as they cautiously exited the alley in the stolen ride.

one

SOMETHING'S COOKIN'

STANDING IN FRONT OF my bathroom mirror, I watched my wife, Khadija, and our live-in girl-friend, Pebbles, still fooling around in bed. Now this ain't something I get all the time, not because I can't, but because I'm always on the go chasing that paper. And just keeping it way real, I don't got the stamina to keep up with thee two of them all of the time if I wanted to.

I observed my wife pull herself away from Peb's sexy lips and then roll out of bed and put on her robe. Khadija's red-brown hair brushed just past her creamy shoulders. She was slim but not model thin with full breasts, a perfect face, and golden-brown eyes that called out to me whenever I stared into them. I watched her walk out of view of the mirror, leaving one behind just as good.

Pebbles's country-thick self-lay spread-eagle masturbating, slowly dipping her fingers in and out of her wetness while motioning me to come back to bed with her with her free hand. Just the thought of the early-morning sex the three of us just had made me ready for another round. Only this time, it was two against one. I stopped what I was doing and climbed back into bed, sliding head-first between her thighs. In one continuous motion I ran my tongue up through her swollen lower lips all the way up to her sweet mouth, pausing to suck and nibble on her excited nipples before I reached my destination. Peb pushed me off of her onto the bed, immediately rolling me onto my back. Then she wrapped her small, soft hand around, took my semihard shaft, and sucked it between her lip's pouty lips. She jagged and sucked me until I was rock hard, then climbed over me and fed my throbbing length into her hot hole. Once she'd buried it balls deep inside her, she leaned down, gave me a passionate kiss, and commenced to riding me. Peb started off slow and long but increased her pace as she rode me. Soon her pace became wild, hard, and shallow, keeping me deep inside her.

You know I could just lie there and let her have her way with me. I tightened my grip on her waist, lifting her up just so and tossing her off of me, but instantaneously flipping her over onto her hands and knees, then plowing back into her wetness from the back. I fucked her hard and fast, trying my

2

hardest to ignore the hot gush as she came repeatedly and the wild moaning of her pleasure and my name into the only pillow left on the bed. Feeling myself about to bust, I quickly withdrew from her box and inserted my cum-soaked hardness into her tight asshole. Now she was really screaming out my name into the pillow as I long stroked in and out of that juicy ass of hers. In no time I shot off inside her and she collapsed.

After standing up in Pebbles's black ass like a man, I had to rush to shit, shower, and dress so I could get my daughter to school on time. I rubbed my hand over my head and beard. It was rough, and I knew it was time for a cut and shave. I'll stop at the shop after I drop Baby off, I told myself, then sang along to Lenny Williams's song "'Cause I Love You" that Khadija blasted on the stereo listening to her favorite morning radio station 98.3 that played all of the R&B and oldies that she loved.

Once out of the shower, I stared in the mirror at myself and smiled. I'm still good and solid for twenty-eight, but I'm always in a good mood in the morning. I know it's a blessing alone just to be able to say that and mean it.

After wiping the baby oil off my hard body, I walked into the bedroom to find it empty, with my outfit for the day laid spread out on the half-made bed. Neither one of my girls had to work today, so I knew they had plans to get right back in it.

I dressed in the maroon-and-tan Polo fit, grabbed my gun and wallet, and went downstairs for a quick breakfast. Pebbles was sitting at the table reading the paper.

The date was Wednesday, October 17, 2012. President Barack Obama and Mitt Romney had their second election debate, and it was front page. I walked up and kissed her like I didn't just see her only moments ago.

"Good morning, you! Where's my Babygirl?" I looked around. "The boys took off already?"

"Morning, bae! You know their bus comes earlier this year, and I ain't seen Nene yet, but she was singing in the shower a moment ago, so she'll be rushing down here in a few," she said without looking from the newspaper.

I looked over her shoulder at the front page of the newspaper and asked, "How did Obama do this time?"

"I told you last night he had ole dude punch drunk from all the blows of his own words he through back at him." She shook her head.

"You know this nigga don't listen to us, Boo. He don't be hearing nothing if it ain't nothing wrong with the kids or us." Khadija grinned at me before kissing me.

"Please don't get her started," I said as she placed a plate in front of me. She had made me a breakfast sandwich of toast, cheese, bacon, and eggs, knowing our Babygirl would be rushing into the dining room, pulling me away from them any moment.

"What kind of bacon is this?" I asked, taking a few bites of the sandwich.

"It's turkey, bae." Dija pointed at Peb, who tried to hide even deeper in the paper.

"Turkey."

"Bae, just give it a chance. I know y'all tell me all the time how much you like my thickness, but I've been picking up weight lately, and I'm not happy with it. Plus, all that pig ain't good for us no way."

What Peb said was true, and I let her know it was okay by finishing my first and asking for another. The girls were all smiles. There was something up with these two this morning. I was going to come home and get to the bottom of whatever it was.

My beautiful Babygirl came rushing down the steps like we knew she would. "Daddy, you finished? Let's go." She looked at my plate. "Let me help you with that." She picked up the other half of my sandwich, taking a bite. "Is this that fake bacon?" She took it off and put it back on the plate. "It taste like cardboard and eggs." She frowned then drained my glass of orange juice.

"I got a few minutes for you to eat that bacon. What you in such a hurry for anyway!"

"Okay, Daddy, no we don't. I'm going to be late. Nisha and Tyshay just text me they outside waiting for us."

"Oh, you in a rush because I told you I would let you drive to school this morning." I smiled.

"Yeah, Daddy, you know me and my girls got to jack on them bum hoes at least once a week so they know their place."

"Bum hoes?" I repeated, looking at Peb and Dija.

"Was? The apple don't fall too far from the tree. Now give our baby the keys," Dija said.

"Okay, she know where the keys at." Before I could finish, she was gone out the door.

Peb walked around the table and handed me both my cell phones. I tried to give her a quick peck on the lips, but she held it longer. Dija walked up and did the same. I had to step back and put the good eye on them, as my grandpops use to say when something was fishy.

"Be safe. Come home for dinner tonight if you can," they said just as I heard Babygirl blow the horn. When I heard the song, I knew she had pulled out her Prada Honda Accord SE.

As I walked out the door, it hit me. "You punks set all this up this morning didn't you?"

"We don't know what you talking about. Too late now, so hurry so they won't be late for school," Dija replied, pushing me toward the door.

I shook my head at myself for letting them trap me into letting our daughter keep this car at school today. I texted my folks Toochie to pick me up from the school. I'm going to take that big step and let her have it on her own one school day. She's fifteen, but she still my baby. As soon as I walked to the car, Toochie texted back, telling me to let the girls go; he should be at my house in two minutes.

"Nisha, you can get in front," I started at Babygirl. "As much as I don't want to do this, I am. You big-head ass girls better go straight to school and don't leave it until it's time to. I ain't playing." Toochie pulled up behind her. "I love you. Be safe!"

"We get to go by ourselves? I love you too, Daddy!" Thank you!" she screamed, then peeled off.

"On a school day? What you been smoking this early, my nigga?" he asked after pulling off behind them after I'd gotten in the truck.

"What, you don't think she ready to be out on her own either, do you?"

"Hey, we got to see what she do. My Nene a good girl. It's that lil black-ass bitch she be fucking with I don't trust around her."

"Man, you just mad because she told yo BM that y'all was fucking on Facebook." I laughed. "You can't be mad at her. You know Irayna came at that girl sideways first. Folks, you know how reckless her mouth is."

"Whatever, nigga. She didn't have to say any that shit. I could've went to jail if the right muthafucka had been online. That lil bitch is bad news. But fuck that. Where we on our way to first?"

"Is Assa at the shop yet? I need to get this shit off my head."

"You know that nigga don't do shit until he feel like it. But if you text him and tell him to let you know as soon as he get there, he will. The nigga won't have us waiting that long" He stopped at the red light. "What are you gonna do for Dija B-day tomorrow?"

"Oh shit!"

"What you forgot?" He chuckled.

"What's today?" I asked, looking at my watch. "That explains what all that funny-acting shit was about at the house just now. Aye, run me to Kay's Jewelers right fast. I need to see what they got in there that I can snatch up for her right quick."

"Why not go to Paks? He can have you right by the morning if you get her a ring or bracelet."

"Hell yeah! That's what I'm going to do. Let's shot there. I'ma grab her both. She been on some shit about a lefthand ring for over two month now anyway. So, yeah, that will work."

"Fam, I'm going to drop myself off at Enterprise since it's right there. I need me a rental so I can be incognito for the weekend."

"What you got up this weekend?"

"If I tell you, I may have to do you in, and then who would I trust with my family gone?" he joked; at least I looked at it that way. After putting a down payment on a cranberry, pineapple, and white diamond complete set—ring, watch, bracelet, and earrings, he threw in another ring for Peb. I'd just spent ten bandz with him before 10:00 a.m. I'd better get something free.

~ ~ ~

I sat down in the barber chair. It was warm in the shop and hot beneath the black nylon barber cloth. The air conditioner hadn't kicked in and did its job yet, but my Glock 23 sat coolly on my lap.

My body welcomed the comfort of the leather chair. I turned my head the way my barber pointed it in. As he did his job, he talked and argued about the Bucks game with an unlit blunt hanging out the corner of his mouth the entire time. That's pretty much all they did in the barbershop—smoke, cut hair, and talk shit, in that order. For the most part the was well respected. There was a few times niggas had come to blows over some petty shit or a female that they were both fuckin' on, but never no gunplay. I still keep my banger with me and ready at all times though.

"How do you want this?" he asked when my head was done.

"Man, you know shit don't change with me."

"I wouldn't be a good barber if I didn't ask." He stepped back and studied my face, brushed out the clippers, and went back to work.

two

MONEY IN, MONEY OUT

I NOTICED IT WAS another unseasonably warm day—scratch that, it was a hot very fall day. I climbed in Toochie's gleaming champagne-colored Escalade and cranked up Young Jeezy on its 15,000-watt stereo system before peeling off into the light traffic.

So, you be in the streets they missing you, welcome back.

Welcome back.

I told y'all I was comin' back.

Welcome back.

I won't let cha have it for long, homie.

Let's go! Welcome back!

Guess who's back and he's shinnin' on you niggas,

Welcome back! Guess who's back and he's stauntin' on you hoes,

Welcome back! Yeah I'm back and I'm shinnin' you niggas,

Yeah I'm back and I'm stauntin' on you hoes,

I been on my grizzie but now I'm back in da place,

And if you show me da money I'll put this brick in ya face,

And if ya ain't got my money I'll put this strap in ya face,

And y'all believing these niggas that's like a slap in the face.

Welcome back!

Guess what I don't give a fuck

None of y'all niggas as real as me pick 'em out line 'em up.

Driving this truck, I couldn't help but think back to when Toochie put me in the game fo' real about ten years back. The story isn't all that gangster gangster. It's dull and simple actually, but I know you wanna hear it, so here it is.

Toochie called me early one morning. "Get up out the pussy and come get yo boy! It's time to get this money. I'm at Denny's off Mayfair Road."

"Folks, ya trippin'. You know I'm already at it," I retorted. "I'm on my way though," I promised, ending the call then tapping the lil broad on the ass who had her head buried in my lap with my shaft in her throat, encouraging her to finish up so I could get on my way. When I got there, he was standing outside next to his black Infinity Q45 smoking on something loud with a sexy snow bunny. "What up, my nigga! I see you out here snowing," I said as soon as he jumped in my passenger seat.

"I see you got jokes this early. But tell me, are you ready to be rich?"

"I'm always ready to do better, my niggas. All you gotta do is tell me wussup."

"We got to go meet up with my plug at that car lot down the street. He's ready to really fuck with ya boy, but he want me to have somebody that can do what I do now to take over for me. He don't need to know how we get down fo' real fo' real, just that I trust you with my life and that you can get the job done."

"You know I got you and I'm always strap, so let's get to it. We can discuss details later."

"Folks, you don't need yo burner for this meet. Don't even bring it in with you."

I started to protest about it but decided to put my life in his hands and placed my gun beneath my seat. Moments later we were being escorted through the showroom of the new and used car dealership to an office in a back room. After I was patted down, just me, Toochie and I was allowed through the door to the office.

"Joe, here's your man, Duda," Toochie introduced us. The man offered his hand to me and I shook it.

"You're Joseph from the commercials on TV," I blurted, a bit surprised that he was the smooth-talking African guy that was all over the TV that we were there to see.

"Yeah. Call me Joe. I like it better," he instructed, flashing his signature smile.

After that early-morning introduction, I haven't turned back since that day. Joe supplied me with all of the heroin and coke I needed. And you already know that I flooded my hood like the Milwaukee river had overflowed. Well that was the simple beginning of it all that I promised you. Whipping through the city now, that shit seemed like a lifetime ago. Especially now, preparing for the day I was gonna make my escape from the dope game.

I made my first stop after the barbershop: my childhood stomping grounds down in B-County on the northeast side of the city. My folks D-Man had been calling me since last night, but once the girls got me home there was no going back out back. Good thing he knew how I operate from our years of dealings. "I'm out front," I said into my cell when he answered my call.

"Dawg man, fuck you! You want me to rush after you took your sweet-ass time getting here."

"That's how you do me? I found myself talking to a deadline with him standing beside my truck's passenger door.

"Wuddup, my nigga?"

"Wuddup, Good thing you came when you did. I'm almost out, and I got another hour until we shut shit down and go to the noon spot. "Here." He handed me a black shopping bag. "This what you get for taking so long to get at me."

I knew right away it was filled with mostly all small bills. I handed him ten ounces of raw heroin, which was his usual order plus four. "Aye, hey! D-Man, it's another four in there I need you to run through for me. I need all the paper off three of them. The other is your for running 'em for me. It's the wife B-Day tomorrow, so I need you to look out for yo boy?"

"I got her. I'll call you ASAP when I got that bread," he replied as he sent a quick text out. "Duda, it's this female that's been riding around selling loud for the dirt. I snatched up two pounds from her last night; it's blowin' on the G! She says that she needs to move what she got a lil faster, so I told her I'll get at you about it."

"You sho she good, G? She ain't them people is she?"

"Ya know I had my bitch give me the rundown on her. She good. Don't even got no unpaid parking tickets."

"Okay, alright, send her to the shop. I'll be there for the rest of the day whenever I make it." D-Man had me pull up on one of his lil guys in the middle of the block, who he passed the pack that I'd just given him off to. Then he had me drop him off at his car parked on the next block. From the Eastside I went up in numbers to the building on Twenty-Seventh and Townsend to pick up and drop all in the same spot. My girl Keys aka LaKisha held down a small stash of drugs and guns for me. Everyone thinks we're fucking, but we're just cool like that. She's like a sister fo' real.

I met Keys five years ago on the bus stop. She'd just missed the bus, and I was sitting at the stop light when it happened. Getting on my good-guy shit, I offered to give her a ride to where she was going or just to the next bus stop. She instantly accepted, getting right in. She explained that she was on her way to a work program that she couldn't afford to be late for. She also vented her frustration about not passing the urine test that was needed for her to be a personal care aid. So I offered her a job taking care of my Pops. His old ass still smokes weed and would love to have a nice ass to look at.

My Pops owned the apartment building I was on my way to as well as lived in it. So to make things easier for everyone involved, I moved her into the vacant unit next door to him. Keys also lived there rent-free. That was the old man's doing. I half-ass suspected that she might be doing some extra special services for him, but, hey, that was between them.

"Where's the old dude at?" I inquired, entering my Pops's apartment.

"He's not feeling well today. He's still in bed asleep." She lowered her voice to a loud whisper. "His ass got a hangover from stealing my bottle of

Remy last night and downing over half the bottle," she said with a little chuckle.

I laughed because I knew how much he loved his Remy. But all his years of drinking and drugging was why she needs Keys around now. "I can hear his old ass in there snoring now," I said, shaking my head. "Have you had any more shit out of them fools down the street?"

"Oh, I didn't tell you?"

"Tell me what?"

"Shit, the police swarmed on them fool-ass niggas the other day. I guess one of 'em jumped on his girl and beat her up real bad, so bad that EMTs called the police. When they arrived she told 'em everythang."

"Damn, that's what they get tryna be on that gorilla shit. I wish we could get them niggas' action online. I know these parts nice."

"Well, I was gonna holla at you about putting Tone on. He has an uncle who lives right on the block over from them, and he gets high, so Tone can work out his crib until you put a spot together for him. All you'll need to do is keep his uncle good. Bro, I got Tone. He won't fuck over me. He don't want me to call you fools on him." She laughed.

"Okay, do you. Let me know when you wanna start and how much you starting him out with. Keys, you know some niggas start acting funny when they start getting paper, especially real paper. I don't want you killing his ass over this move now?"

"I said I got him. I know you don't think I'll let him get too much money without me. Anyway, I already knew you would say it was okay, so I already gave him a sixty-three that I whipped up from a ounce and a half for him to start off with." She put her head down as if I was going to snap.

"You—"

"Duda, I knew you would say okay to me doing it, and I already got the money from him for the whole sixty-three. He thinks he working on our profit right now."

I just shook my head at the thought of how she was working Tone. "Keys, do what you do. I told you, just let me know if you have any kinda trouble outta him. I won't be mad if you do that. Tone don't know that you're holding all that wurk and shit, do he?"

"Oh fuck no! I put it together and had Shawnda come run me to get me some loud to put in the air. That's how Pops got ahold of my drink."

"Alright, keep it that way with Shawnda. Aye, don't her guy sell loud?"

"Yeah, but she don't really fuck with Boo-Man no more. Why you ask?"

"I'm about to go see somebody in a few about some and I'm trying to make it do what it do with it ASAP," I explained as I finished picking up what I needed for my next two stops. "Hey hey hey, Keys. If all goes well see if Shawnda can do the same shit with dude you doing with Tone."

"I was already thinking it. She on her way here now. I'll talk to her about it."

"Okay. Tell Pops I came over and I'll stop back over before I go in the house. I gotta put something nice together for Dija's birthday at the last minute. Can you think of something that I can do real quick like?"

"Nigga, it's tomorrow. How you gonna forget yo wife's birthday, especially with how much she been dropping hints on Facebook?"

"I ain't really been on the Book like that," I lied. I just hadn't been on my page that she knew about.

Wait, before you judge me. It's not like that. I ain't on there tryna fuck with no bitches or no shit. Dija and Peb just don't get along with a few of my friends, and we talk our shit on Facebook to each other, but it's not the way she and Peb make it out to be.

"It's a ladies' night out cruise ship going out tomorrow. Put her on it and rent more time so it'll stay out longer. I'ma call Paul for you and put it together. When I do and get the password, I'll call you with it."

"Thank you! Please do this. You got enough money here to take care of it," I said, hugging and kissing my lifesaver on her cheek before leaving out the door.

"Our outfits on you, too, right, Duda?" Keys yelled behind me.

"Yeah, call if you don't have enough to pay for everything!" I replied, then hit the exit.

three

I BREEZED THROUGH THE hoods handling my business, doing what I do and gettin' that cash. I like to be hands-on with a few of my niggas. But for the others I have someone else handle this shit. I'm playing with my money like a boss should. What I mean by playing is, I bought a lil sandwich shop, and I own a few rental properties and an auto part and repair shop that I'm putting the finishing touches on now for its grand opening. Once I got it up and running good, I'm gone from this street life. Before I made it to Sleepy's Subs, the name of the sandwich shop that I mentioned to you, I placed a call to Toochie to see if he was free to meet me there at that time.

Toochie was what fam went by these days, but growing up he was known to all as Tootie, the name his Big mama gave him. Folks had always been good with money growing up. He just couldn't stay focused in school to get what needed to truly put his money-making gift to use on that next level. Toochie's coffee-brown skin, cocky attitude, solid build, and low brush cut with the waves would almost always have most of the females in whatever room he entered lusting after him, but he never really let it go to his head.

"Wuddup, my nigga, where you at?"

"Shit, I'm here. Where you? Still out looking for something so you don't get fucked up by Dija," he teased with a chuckle.

"Have you forgotten? I'm the truth, nigga? I got that shit under control, fam. You best to chill before I drop this truck off to Classy and she go Rambo on yo fool ass," I shot back.

"Why you want to go there?" We both laughed because we knew how crazy his long-term girlfriend was.

"Aye, just meet me at the shop as soon as you can."

"I'll be there in a few. I'm on my way now as we speak. Say, ask Ariana to tell the new girl to fix me a turkey-and-cheese sub. You know the way I like it. She there, right?"

"Both of 'em there, but I know you know the answer already. G, don't be fuckin' with my staff, and FYI, that girl only seventeen. She just turned it last week I think."

"Hey, I can dream of making seventeen cream, can't I? I'm just joking, but if she fucking, I ain't ducking."

I shook my head when I got off the phone with his ass and made my way to my destination. I had named the sandwich shop Sleep's after my lil cousin who went before his time due a misdiagnosed illness. The place was his dream, and I did my best to dress it up the way he always said he would do it when he got the money. I employed teenagers who needed jobs for school or because they were on probation. Our hours worked with the part-time student. 7:00 a.m. to 11:00 a.m., 11:00 a.m. to 4:00 p.m. and 4:00 p.m. to 9:00 p.m. But I got my young thunder cats to hold it down in the late-night hour 12:00 a.m. to 3:00 a.m. They also kept the spots fed for me in both ways, if you know I mean. I love the smell of freshly baked bread that hits you as soon as you walk in the door. "I'm expecting a female to stop by. When she get here let me know," I told Ariana, my manager. "An' button your shirt up and tuck it in, miss lady. You're at work, not a playhouse," I scolded the new girl as I passed. She quickly did as she was told, and I walked on into my office.

Hours passed as Jamarvya and Toochie ran down their night events. We all sat counting and banding the cash drop from the day before. I'd forgotten about the meeting with the female D-Man had told me about, fooling around with these two knuckleheads and listening to their hoe stories.

"Wuddup?" Toochie exclaimed, answering a knock on the door.

"Ariana told me to tell you the woman you was waiting on is here. Do you want me to bring her back here, or are you coming out?" the feminine voice said through the closed door.

"Shit!" I cursed under my breath, not wanting her or my guest to see all this money out. "Give her something to drink or whatever. Then bring her back here in, like, five minutes," I instructed her.

"You said five minutes? Okay, will do," she confirmed, then asked, "How was the sandwiches?"

"I'll talk to you after you get this done for me," I replied, knowing somebody told her that's how to get on my good side. "Ya, we're gonna have to get back to this here later. Can you go over the books and tell me how much more we need for this week's payroll and put the counters away?"

"Man, Duda, I'm done," Toochie said, standing up from his seat. "You talking like it's finna take you all night with that bitch, and I gotta hit the road in a few with Joe. I'll hit you up to let you know I'm good."

"If y'all about to go, I won't have too much time to get it in the bank in time, so make the payroll unless you just move the money from the other account to cover it," Ya suggested.

I was not too worried about Ya, aka Jamarvya, stealing from me because he got paid very well for what he did. On top of that, my wife Khadija was his big sister. "Okay, whatever, just tell Dija to do that if that's what's needed. I'ma see if this chick worth our time."

"I just went to see what that ass looking like. If she fuckable I might have to have you send her my way, if you don't wanna fuck with her." Toochie would buy swampland if it meant he was going fuck the sexy saleswoman offering it to him. Right then the knock I was expecting came. "Come in," Toochie and I both said at once. When the door opened, this beautiful female walked in. She kinda put you in the mind of Brook from Basketball Wives. I was now standing along with everyone else in the room. Ya and Toochie were staring with a look on their faces. None of my niggas should get caught with over a female. The expression on my face must've been priceless, because the woman was smiling and shaking her head. I quickly composed myself then walked the guys outta the room, immediately closing the door behind them before I spoke.

"D-Man didn't tell me your name. I'm Duda, the person you're here to see."

"D-Man told me that he forgot to tell you my name, but to tell you the truth, he be so damn high that you can't blame him."

I laughed because D-Man not telling me her name was his way of telling me she is who she is without her knowing it. "So, what is it?" I offered my hand.

"Rhonda, but you can call me Queen." She shook my hand. "D-Man didn't tell me too much about you either, but the streets know you, so I found out a lot."

"Seeing that that statement is coming from a woman, I'm going to plea the fifth to whatever you was told," I joked. Now, I've been around dimes all my life. Hell, I got two of the baddest at home. This

Rhonda or Queen was a whole other bread of Badd Bitch. Her hair was cut short and faded on one side of her head with the back feathered up an lightened in just the right places to give her deep brown eyes that dreamy look.

"He told me you would be able to take a nice amount of what I got off my hands. I got a pretty firm price, but for you I may bend a little." As she spoke she opened her bag and lightly tossed a bag of rainbow-colored buds my way.

"It looks good. But how's it smoking?" I inquired as I opened it up and took a whiff of it.

"That's for you. Roll up and you tell me."

"I don't smoke on the clock."

"Like I said, that's for you either way, but I was hoping to do some real business here today and not play games. Just because I'm a female doesn't mean I don't know my shit. I told you from the start, I checked you out, so I know this your place and you can do whatever, whenever. So, either we're doing something or I'm thanking you for wasting my time."

"Hey hey hey!" I quickly cut her off. "I'm not saying that, nothing like it. All I said was I don't fuck around until I'm done with my work. But I got a few of my staff out there that would love to test it out for me and not get in trouble for smoking on the job," I explained to let her know it was all good. Then I called one of my youngsters into the office and told him to get back to me about it right away. After the youngster went off to smoke, a few moments of awkward silence passed between us before her phone sounded off. She paced the room as she talked, and I couldn't take my eyes off her. Queen was thick, and all the way down to her ankles.

"Duda, something just came up. I got to go. Can we get together tomorrow?" she asked me, snapping me out of my head when her call ended.

"Yeah, it's good. You go handle that, and we can just hook up some other time. That loud you got must be some good because the lil nigga didn't come back." We both laughed. "Let me call him quick?" The lil nigga didn't answer none of my calls, so I called Ariana. "Ari, is Badd around you?"

"He on the drive-thru right now. We got a rush just now, so he couldn't get back to you. But if you calling to find out if it was good, shoo we all high off that blunt you gave him. Set me some of that shit aside!"

"I got you, crazy." I hung up. I relayed the
confirmation to Queen with a smile, and she
returned it.

"So, with that can we talk amount and price
when we hook up?"

I agreed and then walked her out to her truck, a
2011 icy-blue Nissan Rogue with a rainbow tint on
its windows. I stood outside and watched her truck
ride out of sight.

"So do I get to know how I did with the sub
now, or is this going to be one of them times I get a
call saying you don't need me?" asked the girl.

"Oh yeah. What's your name so I can stop
calling you the new girl?"

"Tywannie Fields."

"Where you going? I thought you worked until
nine o'clock," I asked, walking her back inside.

"I got some exams at school I got to get to now.
I talked to the manger about it, and she said it was
cool for me to go," she explained nervously.

"Well make sure you do good and bring an
excuse from school when you come in tomorrow."

"Thank you so much! I really needed this job."
She jumped up and hugged me before she rushed
out the door.

four

ALL OF THE DRIVE over to pick up my Mist, my roommate, I couldn't stop thinking of Duda. I tried doing things to take my mind off of him, such as singing along with every song that came over the radio and mentally making plans for my next hairdo. But none of it worked for very long. I promise you that I was so glad when my cellphone rang with my dear roommate's call, because I needed something to take my mind away of my lusty thoughts of him for a bit.

In that office the vibe I felt radiating from him, hummm, was shot right through me. It caused slight sparks to ignite between my thighs. I had to get up and pace the room because the sight of the thick print in his pants of his tool told me I would not be disappointed if I pushed his sexy ass back on the desk and rode him like no tomorrow. The more and more I thought of the way I'd acted, the angrier I got with myself for my behavior. Maybe the man didn't even notice how I was checking him out, and now he thinks I'm a little crazy. Oh well, I know

I'm going to get that money out of the deal before I put this wet wet on him.

"Sooo, did the nigga take any of that bud off our hands? I know I'm gonna be a broke bitch after I pay for my car to be fixed," Mist stated after her inquiry while lying her back against the headrest once she'd settled into the passenger seat of my car.

During the drive to the gentlemen's club that Mist works at from time to time named On the Border because it borders two cities in the state, I filled her all in about the man and my meeting with Duda. I even told her about the brief sexual energy I'd felt just being around him. She listened to me, smiling and shaking her head. When I was done, she sighed and chuckled.

"Why you do all that?" I questioned as I turned into the parking lot and found a nice parking spot by the entrance. Once there I'd instantly decided that I was going inside the raunchy establishment for a much-needed shot of tequila or three.

"Bitch, you need some dick!" Mist blurted out, then laughed until tears fell.

"Fuck you, hoe!" I retorted, but she was right. It had been too long. My last time was with my son's father, James, and it had now been more than two years since I had lost them both to a house fire. So Mist was right in her teasing. It wasn't just because of Duda with his flawless swagger and hard body.

Approximately an hour later at home now, after downing enough tequila shots to make me dance topless on the stage after one of my sexy roommate's sets, I took me a hot shower to wash off the dirty shameful feeling that I had after the night's behavior. The hot water beating on my skin only returned my thoughts to Duda. I found my hands lingering in places longer than they needed to be. In no time my fingers were doing a dance between my thighs that made my body quake. When the much-need climax was over, I quickly ended my shower and dressed for bed. "Sleep will make it better," I told myself. I soon found out that I was so wrong.

~ ~ ~

When I arrived back home, Dija was the only one there.

"Where is everybody at, sexy?" I asked as I entered the room where she sat watching an unfamiliar TV show.

"Peb had Coco drive her to the YMCA. You know her Zumba workout class is tonight," she answered me over her shoulder, not missing a moment of the ending of her show. "Don't worry, Peb had Coco drop her off so she would have to come back to pick her up, and hopefully won't be late getting in this house." Dija stood up, and I noticed that she was dressed in a shark blue-and-gray dress and leggings. "Now before you get started about Coco and that car, bae, she only got a half day of school tomorrow because of testing, so we let her and her friends take it and hang out a bit to give their minds a break from all of the hard studying that they've been doing."

"What makes you think I was gonna say something about the car?" I asked, walking closer to her. Looking in her eyes, I was feeling a little sting of guilt that I didn't understand because I'd done nothing wrong.

"Because I know you. And thank you so much for the birthday party cruise with the girls," she said excitedly, kissing me. "Bae, what makes you think that I don't wanna be with you too?"

"Who said you want to be with me? The party don't start until later. That gives us a whole day to be together."

"Stop it, bae, You know you're not gonna miss a day working for nothing."

"You're not nothing, Khadija. You're my wife. The better half of me, and the one I love, right?"

"Yes, I am, and you don't forget it!" She kissed me, and I passionately returned it.

My mind rushed to Queen, and I quickly suggested, "Let's go out to eat right now. Just the four of us."

"You know they going to be mad at us for going out to eat without them."

"Whatever. One is working out, so she don't need to eat, and the other is roaming the streets aimlessly just to be seen driving. Ain't nobody thinking about us."

"The boys ate already. They're in their room getting ready for bed. I told them they could finish the game they were playing. They bad asses think that I don't know they started it over," she explained with a small chuckle. "Let me go in there and tell them we're about to go and to go to bed."

After Dija got the boys settled, she got herself together quickly by removing the leggings and teasing her hair. We ended up at the Olive Garden laughing and talking over our delicious two for $25 meals. Afterward we headed down to Bradford Beach, where we walked hand in hand on the lakefront. In my head I asked myself why I was tripping over another woman when I had what I had right here. My cell phone beeped letting me know I had a text and snapping us out of our moment.

As I read, Dija said, "I know you gotta go, bae, but when we get home, can I get some before you do."

The text was from Ariana telling me she picked up the pieces that I bought from Pak's and put it on top of the old cooler. "Hell yeah, you can get this! I just gotta make a stop first, and then I'm yours." On our drive home, we finished off the bottle of wine that was left over from our dinner.

Once home, as quietly as we could, we tipsily tiptoed through the house, making our way into our bedroom. Right through the door our clothes went flying every which way. On the bed, Peb was sound asleep, obviously worn out from her workout. Seeing her partly covered breast and her leg sticking from under the covers did something to the both of us.

I woke her by placing my soft kisses on her forehead, eyes, and lips as I fondled her breast, lightly pinching her nipple. Khadija helped with her firm kisses to Peb's thighs, butt, and unshielded lower lips. Peb pushed me away and pulled Dija from between her legs to her face. I got down and right away filled her hot hole with my hard thickness. As I hammered into her, she pulled Dija up over her face. Leaning back against my chest, me and Dija kissed while Pebbles simultaneously licked and sucked Dija's clit. As soon as I felt them cumming together, I knew I would not be going any farther than business with Ms. Queen. I pushed Dija down on top of Peb and pulled right out of Peb's hot wet hole only to drive right into Khadija's, where I almost instantly climaxed, filling up the warmth of my loving wife.

five

IT CAN'T BE SO

PULLING UP ON THE hot Eastside I instantly
texted D-Man and let him know that I was about to
be pulling up. I didn't want to be sitting outside
waiting on him too long. It wasn't long before a
grimy-looking, tatted-faced, light-skinned kinda
sexy dude began to approach my window. Before I
made it, D-Man exited the house and shooed him
away with a wave of his hand then hopped in
with me.

"So how did shit go wit' my nigga the other
day?" D-Man inquired immediately after we'd
concluded our business before getting out of
my truck.

"It went good. We're suppose to be hooking up
in a few. I'm hoping he take a nice amount of this
bud off my hands, because I'm gettin' sick of it
now."

"You sick of it? Shit, all you gotta do is give it
to me!" he joked and grinned.

"Yeah, whudeva, D-Man." We laughed. "I did put you a lil somethin extra in there for the lookout with your guy though."

"Alright, alright, that's wussup! You ain't about out yet, is you?" he questioned with a hint of panic in his voice.

"Not even close. But you know when it's gone, it's gone. I'm done."

"Yeah, yeah, I know," he mournfully replied, "Alright, I gotta put this in motion. I'ma hit you when I need you," he promised before getting on out then jogging back inside the house.

As I made my way back toward my house, I thought of Duda. It wasn't just money that had him on my mind. It was everything. I really wanted to see him. When my cell phone suddenly began playing the ringtone that I'd programmed for Duda, my heart skipped a beat. I hurriedly retrieved my phone from my bag and answered.

"Hello, hi!" I hoped my voice didn't give my anxious thoughts away. I know it did from the short hesitation before Duda spoke.

"Queen?. Is this you?"

"It's me. I'm trying to concentrate on driving," I said, tryna make an excuse for the way I sounded answering the call. "You ready to see me already?"

"Yes and no."

"What do you mean?"

"I'm getting twenty-five pies off you at full price, but I can't make it to do the deal with you."

"Why? Is something wrong? I can wait on you. I don't want to fuck with a dude I don't know."

"I know you don't. That's why I'm having my manager Ari take care of you for me. You do remember her, right?"

"Yeah, I remember her. That will be fine. So can we still get together for drinks later?" I sounded desperate.

"I don't think that would be a good thing tonight."

"Why? What you scared of?" I flirtatiously teased.

"It ain't like that. I just can't make it. I forgot I got a little get-together to go to tonight."

Wow, if I didn't want to give the nigga the pussy, he would've been all over me. But here I was fighting myself not to, and this muthafucka ducking me. On top of it, the fifty thousand that he'd tossed my way only fucked my head up even more. I'd hoped at the most he would buy ten off me for a deal of fifteen, geez, but twenty-five at my price for each—I couldn't believe it. I shook off my disappointment some, ended the call with him, and then placed a call to Mist to get the order ready. "Bitch, wake your ass up and start getting dressed! Shit, are you even at home yet?"

"Yeah, I'm here, wuddup?"

"Good, now get twenty-five of them ready for me so when I get there we can go right away."

"Whole ones?"

"That's what I said."

"For ole boy, what's his name?"

"Yep. As a matter of fact, throw a couple extra in there for him since he paying full price."

"Full price! Bitch, what you do to that man to make him spend that type of money?"

"I wish, but I didn't do shit. We're not even doing the deal with him. He got us meeting up with some bitch that works for him."

"Bitch, is you mad?" She laughed. "Let me find out."

"I was looking forward to seeing him, I ain't going to lie. He made up some lame-ass excuse about having a get-together to go to so he couldn't be there to do it himself."

"Oh shit! I almost forgot to tell you. The nigga married, and he's the one who chartered that boat you going on tonight."

"How did you find that out? And it's a ship not a boat."

"Whuteva, you won't catch my black ass on it. I seen the movie The Perfect Storm. Anyways, it's like five or six girls from the club going to perform for her."

"So, what you're tellin' me is that his bitch goes both ways?"

"I don't know. But I also heard that she use to dance herself a few years ago and that's how they met, from what I've been hearing."

"I'm almost there, so be looking out for me," I told her as I immediately ended the call and sped up, fuming mad with myself wondering how I could compete. I know one thing for sho, I wouldn't be missing that cruise later.

six

LET'S GET THIS MONEY

MIST GLANCED AT THE clock on her car radio and seen that it was a little after one o'clock in the morning. Her and another girl dancer that worked with her at the strip club had set up dates earlier that evening with some guys that had promised them a big payoff for a private show.

"I bet I should've went on that boat tonight. I know them bitches going to be paying good."

"They might be, but you gotta look at how many girls went," Mist replied. "Bitch, we would be lucky to walk away with $200 each at the end of the cruise, but fuckin' with these niggas we're gettin' $500 each just to show up, plus tips on top of that."

"Gurl, are you sure they got the money?"

"Let me find out. You don't know who Joe or Toochie is?" Mist asked, and Kustom sat there with a blank clueless expression on her face. "Ooooh, wow! Bitch, you is green," she exclaimed shaking her head in disbelief. "I got this car from the nigga Joe's car lot, and all I put down was a lil poo poo."

"He gave you this Lexus for some pussy? I hope he got another one he wanna give away!" Kustom said, surprised by Mist's confession. "But let me guess, he's your personal, right?" she asked, zipping up her black sateen and leather thigh-high boots.

"Nawl, it ain't like that. Toochie is his right hand, and he also a rich boss nigga in these streets. The young nigga with them is one of their close guys I guess. I dunno. Just play yo cards right and anything can happen," Mist told her, then used the downtime that they had to give her the rundown of all she knew about the guys they were planning on doing the private show for, as well as what was expected of them when they got there.

What she didn't tell her was she had plans on charging her for letting her in on the show. Mist picked Kustom out of all of the rest of the girls in On the Border. One, because she had a good feeling that Toochie as well as the others would go wild over Kustom's tall, thick, curvaceous body. And, two, Mist knew that once the party started, the naive girl would do it all for a buck.

By the time she finished hyping her up, the guys had arrived. Mist followed the men to Joe's main car dealership, where they got comfortable on the

second floor above the showroom. Badd already
had a bottle open and a blunt lit by the time the door
was unlocked.

"We got y'all for the rest of the night, right?" he
asked, then gave Mist butt a soft tap.

"You got us for as long as your paper goes, lil
daddy," Kustom told him, giving him a flirtatious
wink that ended with a mischievous smirk on her
sexy glossy lips.

"You bitches won't ever leave this bitch fucking
with us then, shawty!" Toochie jacked as he
retrieved a big bankroll from his pocket and tossed
half of it on the table and the other half in the air
above their heads.

"No, no, homey, tonight on me. I'm gonna pay
for this here lil party out of my petty cash pot," Joe
said, then reached into his desk drawer and removed
a lock box. Once he found the correct key and
opened it, he nonchalantly tossed the girls a stack
each. "We get no holds barred for that, right?" he
asked lustfully, eyeing Kustom.

"Almost," Mist responded, collecting both her
and Kustom's money and placing it in her bag. "Is it
a place we can go get ready?"

The office space they were standing in was more of a fuck pad than anything. It had a small bedroom with a full-size bed, a hideaway bed in the sitting room, and a full private bathroom. The night was an easy one for Mist. By the time her girl-on-girl preshow was over, Joe was too intoxicated for much of anything more. Plus, Toochie and Badd and the other guy that was there really wanted to fuck on the sexy foreign girl. It wasn't that she was better-looking than Mist. It was that she was an attractive mixture of British and Nigerian, and the sound of her voice drove them wild. Pretty much as soon as Kustom stood up from between Mist's legs, the guys began to feel her up. Right then Mist decided that she would let them have at her while she went into the other room to tend to her wealthy sugar daddy's needs.

Giving Kustom an encouraging head nod, Mist stood and pulled Joe into the next room, leaving her alone with the other three men. Kustom didn't cringe nor hesitate. She almost instantly dropped down and went to work on their semihard lengths. The little foreign slut bucket was able to deep throat Badd's and the other guy's shafts but could only take in half of Toochie's long, thick girth. When she had them all throbbing hard, she got on the sofa bed, which Toochie had immediately pulled out when he saw Kustom start putting her pretty mouth to work on his two guys. On the bed bent over on her knees sucking and jerking the two erections in front of her off, she felt Toochie poking his finger into her hot, wet hole.

After getting his finger nice and coated with her juices, he put it into her asshole and begin to work it in and out of her. He increased the pace of his finger fucking as well as the number of fingers that he was pushing inside of her. When he had Kustom's asshole loosened enough to accept three of his thick fingers, Toochie withdrew them and eased his hardness in her in their place. He felt Kustom begin cumming instantaneously and took a moment to enjoy the feeling of her body's tremble from the orgasm entering her asshole caused. Before long she'd collected herself and found a good rhythm that allowed her to please all three of the guys at once.

In the next room Mist stood in front of Joe naked, watching him ogle her mouthwatering breasts' stiff nipples as he took off his pants. What made fucking Joe so easy was his size. Even semihard, his length was big, and as soon as it was free from his boxers, she was down on her knees. She licked it until it was fully awake. Then it was so big that she almost couldn't get her mouth around it completely. Mist sucked him while simultaneously playing with his balls for about two good minutes straight before he shoved her lips off of him, then scooped her up and tossed her onto the bed. Then he feverishly began kissing her and sucking on her dime-size nipples. After a while he moved his lips downward until his tongue expertly teased her clit. Mist spread her legs nice and wide, allowing him to feast on her for over five minutes, giving her a series of tiny orgasms minute after minute. Mist had her eyes closed enjoying the pleasure she was getting. Soon she felt Joe's tip parting her warmth and its girth stretching her hole as he pushed into her. Joe pinned her to the bed, holding her down by her throat as he mercilessly fucked her. Mist thrust with him, throwing it back at him showing him that she could give it as well as she could take it. She came hard and harder as he was ramming his hardness deeper and deeper still for about fifteen minutes straight before bringing her to a screaming

climax right after he'd shot off into her wet
wet box.

Mist put it on Joe just the way he liked her to.
And after he passed out, she freed herself from his
arm and went to look in on Kustom to see how she
was doing with the bunch. The four of them were
still going strong. Kustom was fucking and sucking
with a look of pure delight on her face. Seeing that
she did need her assistance, Mist headed on down
the hall to the soda vending machine. On the way
there, Mist noted that for Kustom to be so green in
the hoe game, she was way advanced in the right
areas to make it work for her.

~ ~ ~

"You good, Ya? I'ma take off now so I won't be
late pickin' my mom up from the airport," Ariana
said, gathering her things to leave.

"Yeah. Who's still out front with you?" Ya
called from the office where he was finishing up the
last of the payroll.

"Tywannie, James, and Breanna. The others
ain't got here yet, but they called and said they're
on their way on the bus."

"Alright then, I'll stay 'til they get here. See
you tomorrow."

After Ari went home for the night, things slowed down a bit, so Tywannie and the others decided to clean the line and kitchen. "Ya, could you shut off the back door alarm so I can take the trash out?" Tywannie asked.

"Okay, give me a second to finish this." Ya finished locking up the office and then went and disarmed the back door so Tywannie could get to the dumpster and him to his car. "Tywannie, let me help you with that." He grabbed two of the trash bags from her.

"Thanks!" She followed him with the third.

Neither of them saw the dark-dressed man until he stepped from the shadows with his gun in his hand. "Don't move! Keep ya hands so I can see them." He pointed his gun in Ya's direction as he walked up.

"Run!" Ya ordered Tywannie, but pushed her so hard that she lost her footing and fell inside the doorway. Quickly, Ya drew his gun and shot twice. The man screamed out in pain and ducked back behind the dumpster. He heard Ya's footsteps coming his way and others coming to see what was going on. The would-be robber sprang from his hiding place, shooting wildly as he ran for the fence that separated the lot from the dark alley. Ya dived out of the way of the shots and returned some of his own. But the man was over the fence and sprinting away. Ya ran over and stood at the fence, trying to catch a glimpse of the attempted robber, but a few moments later all he heard was a car peeling off down the dark alley.

"Ya, you alright?" asked Fame as Lil Mike helped him up. They had just made it when they heard the shooting.

"Yeah, I'm good. Where is Tywannie?"

"I'm right here," she responded from the doorway with Bree and James. "Do you want me to call the police?" she asked.

"No, need. They're shit. I don't think he gonna come back." He saw her limping from the door when they walked back inside. "You alright? What's hurt?"

"I hit my knee when I fell in the doorway."

"Fame, y'all got this, or should I just close up for the night?"

"Naw, fam, we good. I ain't going to let that lil shit scare us into closing up. I got my burner on me. We good. You can get outta here."

"Alright. Bree, get Tywannie's stuff for me."

"Why? I'm good. I can work."

"No, you can't. Just take the rest of the night off. I don't want you standing on that leg. I'll drop you off at home."

"Here, girl, put this on your knee." Bree handed her an ice pack and her book bag.

"Thanks!"

Fame and the others walked them back out to Ya's car. Once they pulled safely out of the parking lot, they went back inside and back to business.

Pulling up in front of Tywannie's house, Ya asked, "Do you need help up the steps?"

She tried to stand, and pain shot down her leg. "Yeah, I think it's swollen now." He carried her up the short flight of stairs to the door. She got out her keys and gave them to him to unlock the door. He helped her inside. "Thank you!"

"No problems. I want you to take the next few days off so that leg can heal up. Don't worry, I'll pay you for them still, okay?"

"Okay, thanks!" When he turned to leave, she grabbed his hand and stopped him.

"What up?" he asked, and she answered by pulling him toward her and kissing him. "What was that about?"

"It was my thank-you for saving me tonight, and I really like you, Ya. Did you hear what I said?"

"Tywannie, I like you, too, but you're too young. I ain't tryna catch a case like that."

"I'm grown. I'm nineteen. You not that much older than me. Do I got to show you my ID?"

"Yeah, let me see it." She showed it to him. "Duda told me you were younger."

"How old are you? Twenty, twenty-one?" she guessed.

"I'm twenty-three."

"Like I said, not too much older. Chill with me for a minute. I stay here with my sister, and she at work right now."

"I got a few things to do tonight, and I gotta tell Duda what happened. But we can get together later when yo leg is better."

"Alright, call me."

"I will."

This time he kissed her then walked back to his car smiling like a cat with a ball of yarn.

seven

PARTY POOPERS

THE BEDROOM DOOR SMASHED open just as Joe was getting up to use the bathroom, but before he could register the bang of the door slamming into the wall, Joe was being violently knocked to the floor. Fighting the best, he could, Joe crashed to the floor, taking one of the armed masked men down with him. Joe threw his fist wildly, coming to the realization that he was in a robbery. Two of his blows connected with the jaw of the assailant. Then Joe immediately rolled onto his knees and sprang to his feet. Covered in the masked man's blood from the nose-breaking slug he gave him, he tried to make a run for it.

~ ~ ~

In the other room Badd and Toochie were too deep into their fuck fest to pay attention to the added commotion until they heard the sudden boom of the first gunshot. Immediately Badd sprang into action, grabbing his gun and pants at the same time. Toochie followed the goon's lead, quickly getting dressed as he cursed himself for not having his gun on him.

"What's happening?" Kustom frantically demanded as she took cover on the floor beside the bed.

"Stay down! Stay down!" Badd ordered, racing away from her and practically face-to-face with one of the masked invaders. Spotting the gun, Badd promptly raised his gun and dumped a shot in the intruder's direction.

The stun robber fired back as he dove out of the way. Two of his shots hit Badd in the upper body, and at the same time Badd's shot struck the masked man on the outer side of his thigh, knocking him to the floor. Quickly getting back onto his feet, the assailant put a finishing shot in Badd for his pain.

Toochie had instantly begun looking around for something to arm himself to fight with before the door flew open.

"Nooo! God noo!" Kustom screamed as the robber turned his weapon on her and squeezed the trigger.

Toochie flung a chair as hard as he could at the gunman, then sprinted for the exit, plowing his shoulder into the masked man at full force. They both hit the floor hard. Toochie pounded him with a few hard elbows and side fists, then jumped to his feet in hopes of getting his hands on the fallen gun. That's when a sudden boom boomed.

~ ~ ~

Mist couldn't stop herself. As soon as she heard the gunfire, she took off franticly, racing toward it instead of away, slowing to a light jog when she neared the bedroom. Through the smashed door, she spotted the lifeless body of Joe and then a masked man rummaging through the room, tossing and flipping furniture. Without a second thought, Mist grabbed a heavy brass lamp, and swinging it with all her might, she bashed him in the back of his head with a hit. Instantly he went down, twitching on the floor. She snatched up his gun and then ran toward the next room with only two things on her mind: Get Kustom and get the two of them out of there.

When she saw Toochie spring up from the floor running toward her, she took aim, firing twice and striking the masked man chasing behind him.

"What the fuck is going on?" she demanded.

Toochie slowed long enough to pick up another gun. "Let's get out of here. We can talk when it's safe," he exclaimed, taking her hand and towing her back in the direction she had come.

"Where's Kustom?" she questioned, not really wanting to hear the answer he had for her.

"She didn't make it," he informed her once they were inside the car.

"Fuck! Fuck! Fuck! My bag has my ID and shit in it!" she told him, thinking fast.

"If you don't got shit to do with this, you don't got shit to worry about. But, bitch, I don't give a damn. We ain't goin' back until the police say so."

"What nigga, you calling the police?" Mist asked in surprise.

"I gotta. I'm part owner of that place, and our things are all over the place," he explained, then pressed the OnStar button reporting what had happened as soon as the first responder answered.

~ ~ ~

I sat slouched in my plush leather office chair trying hard to center my thoughts. Struggling inside, I rolled up some of the buds that I'd purchased from Tereka and put it in the air along with my stress. That woman had me doing the opposite of my norm. Like now, here I was at work with a blunt burning between my lips. I was feeling so torn that, once again, I let Jamarvya handle the count on his own. Somehow the day had crept by without another thought of the beauty, with Dija and Pebbles getting themselves together for her birth bash. I was left alone studying the blueprints of the inner layout of the auto parts and repair shop.

My cell rang the ringtone I'd set for the contractor. "Jerry, wudd it do! I was just sitting here looking over these blueprints."

"I'm good, Marqsheo. Aye, do you have any plans fo' tonight? I was thinkin' dinner? We can talk about whuteva changes you got on yo mind then."

"Ahh, man, tonight's my wife's birthday party, and I plan to surprise her by attending. She don't know I'm in town right now."

"Nigga, let me find out that you're about to jump outta a cake dressed in only whipped cream, a thong, an shit!" he teased, laughing at himself.

We both laughed. "Nawl, nigga, none of that! But it sho sounds like you've been thinkin' 'bout doin' that there," I retorted, then asked, "Where you at?"

"I'm here in the Mil. I got that contract to remodel Thirty-Eighth Street's school thanks to you. Felisha came with me to spend some of the money I just made by going out shopping with her cousin. It was her who said we should have a dinner party like the white folks."

"Well, we can get together then."

"That's wussup! It can't be that late no ways because we gotta be at the airport by 9:30 p.m. tonight," Jerry said, then told me where to meet them at and we got off the line. It was dusky outside, and I really ain't in the mood to be bothered with him, but I had to be cordial with him. After all, he's helping me make my dream come true, plus he should have some cash for me. I freshened up and then dressed in True Religion jeans and a crisp white soft cotton matching button up, and coco brown Louis Vuitton loafers. I brought it all together by getting moderately icy, adding my platinum big-face diamond Rolex and equally icy Rolex bracelet. After giving myself a once-over in the mirror, I grabbed my phones and then made my way to the restaurant.

Once there I handed the valet the key to my ride and then strolled on in. Just inside the entrance of the classy restaurant I was stopped by its maître d'. I gave my name and told her that Jerry and Felisha were expecting me. She gave her guest list a quick scan, then waved a waitress over to escort me to my friends. Jerry stood up when he spotted me. I shook his hand and then gave Felisha a nod and smile. She did the same.

"You know, whenever I see you, I think of the actress Stacy Dash," I told Felisha.

"Hummm, I guess that means I look good?"

"No, just clueless," I said, teasing her, and we all shared a laugh. Right away I noticed that there was another placement at the table. I guessed it was for Felisha's cousin, but I still asked them to be sure. "Who's missing?"

"Nobody, here she comes now," Felisha answered.

I followed her eyes. I think we saw each other at the same time. I hesitated but still stood up to greet her when she got to the table. "You must be the cousin I've been hearing about?"

"And you're the Mr. Marqsheo I've been told about," Queen said, matching my politeness.

There was a glow in her eyes. "It's good to see you again so soon," I whispered.

~ ~ ~

I tried to hide my surprise, but, what is he doing here? I asked myself. Jerry knows a lot of people, so Duda being here shouldn't have surprised me. I hoped he didn't think the guy Jerry was waiting for was with me whenever he arrived.

"Marqsheo, this is Rhonda," Felisha introduced him. I was even more surprised. Duda said something to me, but something in me was so glad to see him I really didn't hear him. I couldn't help but think of how good it would be to kiss him, to taste him. Like a true gentleman, he pulled my chair out for me.

"Thank you!" I said, sitting down. Felisha leaned in my ear and asked me what she had missed. "Not now," I told her and took a sip of my lemon water.

~ ~ ~

The night was still pretty warm even out in the middle of Lake Michigan. Pebbles inhaled a few deep breaths of the night air.

"Happy birthday, baby. I love you!" she exclaimed before kissing Dija. Peb noticed that Khadija's hands were slightly trembling as she held them.

"Thank you! I love you more!" They stood on the ship's deck greeting all her friends, coworkers, and others who bought tickets for the party cruise.

At 10:45, the DJ played Juicy J's song, "Bandz a Make Her Dance," and the captain came over and informed them he was about to be pulling out for the first-hour cruise before her party got started full force. Dija didn't know it, but this was all a part of the play to sneak me on board. On this first round out, everyone danced and drank, danced some more, and drank. Two of the strippers on board fooled around with the captain as he tried to concentrate on navigating the large yacht. A long-legged white girl dressed in a skimpy red-and-white cheerleader uniform, complete with her long hair pulled up in a flowing ponytail on top of her head, dropped to her knees in front of the captain. Then she began seductively nibbling and biting on the nearly hyperventilating man's crotch as she unzipped his pants with her teeth.

"I've never sucked a captain off at work before. Let's see if you can drive this big ole thing while I see how much of this one I can fit down my throat," she said, taking him deep into her warm mouth.

The captain hadn't in a million years expected anything close to this to be happening to him. It was truly one of his freaky fantasies come true. He'd tried many times in the past to have his wife suck him off while he was at the wheel, but she would always refuse him the pleasure. Now he had a pretty young tender slut who just may be the same age as his daughter swallowing his dick. Her warm wet mouth felt like a slice of heaven to him. The captain felt no shame as his eyes rolled from the blissful blowjob.

~ ~ ~

Some fools decided to race by starlight on the dark, choppy waters of Lake Michigan, filled with Yukon Jack, cocaine, and Bud Lite. One of the drunken racers pushed his speed boat to its max, almost immediately crashing into a wave. Panicking, he lost control of the boat, violently sideswiping the other speed boat, sending it airborne just as the yacht came into view. The distracted captain couldn't react fast enough, and the collision with the airborne speedboat sent them exploding into a big ball of flame and smoke.

"Oh my God! Nooo!" Ariana screamed from the lake's dock, where she and a few other late partygoers waited for the party ship's return.

eight

HEARTBREAK

WHEN DINNER WAS OVER, my cousin and I excused ourselves from the table and went to freshen up in the restroom, leaving the men to finish taking care of whatever business they needed to take care of. Once out of earshot of the guys, I confessed to Felisha what I was feeling for Duda, or Marqsheo, as she knew him. All the while I talked she was fixing her makeup in the restroom mirror.

"Ask him to drive you home. That way you'll have some alone time with him. Then, bitch, go for what you know. He's a man. He's not going to turn you down two times. Hell, I'm very surprised it happened the first time."

"Okay, bitch, I'ma try it," I said, deciding to take her suggestion. "Now come on, you look fine." I pulled her away from the mirror and out the restroom door. When we returned to the table, the men were standing.

"Rhonda, do you mind if my man here takes you home so we won't have to rush to the airport?"

Jerry asked, putting on his "you can't say no to this" smile.

"No, I don't mind," I answered without hesitation. Duda nodded at me, showing his sexy dimples. What's he doing to me?

"Okay." Felisha smiled. "Gurl, I'ma call you from the airport, or should I wait until we get home to call?" she asked, giving me a wink. I kicked her in the foot.

A few minutes later, we were all saying our goodbyes and making promises to get together again soon. Outside of the restaurant there was some type of issue that had the police involved, so Duda and Jerry were given the choice of going to get their own vehicles from the parking lot or waiting until the situation was taken care of. That was an easy choice for us. I walked with Duda to his car. We didn't speak to one another during the stroll. I kinda sensed that he was as nervous as I was. For the second time that night, Duda acted gentlemanly by opening the door for me before briskly walking around and dropping into the driver seat. He pressed the ignition button, bringing the car to life along with the sound of the '90s group,

Xcape being played by radio station 98.3. When he reached to change it, I touched his hand to stop him.

"Wait, I love this song. Let me hear it," I pleaded.

"What you know about Xcape?"

"I know I like this song and that TI's wife, Tiny, use to be in the group," I responded with a little sass as we pulled off into the crowded night traffic.

"So where are we going?"

Anywhere you wanna take me, was my thought. "Oh, I live on Seventy-Second and Bluemound Road," I answered, laying my head back on the headrest of his soft leather seats.

~ ~ ~

I lit up the rest of the blunt I'd been puffing on before I went to the restaurant and blew it, zipping through the streets heading toward Queen's house. She turned to me. "Is that some of mama's best?"

"Sure is," I replied, instantly passing it to her. I watched the glow of the blunt light up her face. Her eyes were dreamy when she looked at me. "I didn't expect to see you again."

"Are you happy you did?"

"Honestly, I don't know how to answer that. I might be walking into something."

"Might be," she flirted, then turned up the radio.

I let myself get lost in the moment by putting my arm around her shoulder when she leaned on me. When we were just minutes from her crib, she sat up and said, "Come in and sit a bit. I won't bite anything you don't want me to."

"Funny, ha ha! I need to use your bathroom anyway. And just so you know, I bite back," I replied, parking in front of her place. She blushed and got outta the car. I followed behind her watching her hips sway and her ass jiggle as we walked up the stairs leading into her house. Inside I was impressed by her taste and cleanliness.

"Do you want a drink? I got beer, Patron, and Remy," she named off.

"I'll take a beer and a shot of Remy. Where's the bathroom?" She pointed to a door just off the kitchen. I knew I shouldn't be here, but I strongly felt a need to see what was all to her, especially now that we had run into each other like this.

~ ~ ~

I kicked off my heels and then fixed our drinks when he went to use it. Already feeling the effects of the wine and weed I'd already consumed before we to my place I was good and in the mood to get fucked. I mean hard sweaty fucking, if I'm being honest. I want Duda to catch me up what I've been longing for. A few minutes later he returned and we went into the front room.

"I need to get out of this dress do you mind?"

"No, go right ahead."

"Can you unzip me please?" I asked, standing and turning around. I could feel his eyes on my ass and when he touched me to free me from my dress. I couldn't help myself. I spun around and kissed him. When he didn't kiss me back, I pulled away. "I've been wanting to do that all night. I'm sorry if I'm being too forward for you."

He answered by pulling me to him and pushing my dress on off. I let it fall right there to the floor. This time he pulled me to him, kissing me with a wanting I knew we both shared. I feverishly undid the buttons of his shirt down to his belt while sucking on his lips and tongue.

~ ~ ~

Queen was even more sexy standing before me in only her bra and panties. We kissed as she worked at getting my clothes off. When she had my shirt open and my belt and pants undone, she suddenly stopped kissing me, but didn't make me wonder what was next. She took my hand and led me into her bedroom. Once inside she hit a button on a remote that filled the room with soft music, then got comfortable on the bed and watched me finish undressing myself.

As soon as I stepped out of my pants and climbed on top of her, both of my cell phones went off, playing the ringtones for Ari and my daughter. "Fuck! My bad, gotta answer that."

"It's okay, answer it."

I shared the disappointment that I heard in her voice. "Wuddup, Ari?" I answered her call because I'd missed my daughter's.

"You gotta get here now, Duda! Please, please hurry, Duda. They blew up!"

She was talking fast and crying. She was so distraught that I couldn't really understand what she was trying to tell me. "Slow down, calm down. Ariana, what are you talking about?" I could hear a lot of people and noise in the background. "Where are you?"

"Duda, I'm at the docks. The party boat just blew up with everybody on it."

The words hit me hard, but I couldn't believe them. "I'm on my way. Call Coco back for me but don't say nothing to her. Tell her I said to stay over Nu Nu house."

"Is there anything I can help you with?" Queen asked just as her own cell began ringing. She sent the caller to voice mail.

"No, I gotta go. It's a. an emergency."

"Wait, just wait, Duda. You're shaking and look like you seen a ghost. Please tell me what's wrong. I'm here for you."

I for some reason knew she was telling the truth. I told her what I was told as we got dressed and rushed out of the house.

nine

CADILLAC SAT BACK OBSERVING the hot new girl who danced under the named Kustom, gyrating her ass as she worked her way around the club, bouncing from table to table. Cadillac was no different from everyone else in the strip club. He longed to be buried balls deep between her sexy glitter-coated legs. But he couldn't work on bringing his fantasy of fuckin' Kustom to life until he got what he was there for, which wasn't sexual pleasure.

The hot-tempered thug had been out of jail for three days now, and for the past two nights he and his two goons had been posted up inside the club looking for Cadillac's ex-girlfriend with no luck. Now on his third night there, he knew his bad luck had changed when The DJ announced the next dancer to the stage. Just hearing the mention of the pretty seductress's name made his length throb. Watching her swing herself around the pole with a skilled steadiness, he thought back on the last time he and Mist were together to keep him focused on the reason the three of them were there.

Approximately two months earlier, Cadillac sat in the club just as he was doing now, watching Mist working. For some reason he wasn't feeling all of the time she was spending bumping and grinding on Joe and his clique. Sure, they tipped her good for her performance, but in his mind Mist was doing too much touching and giggling with them.

Cadillac was suppose to be working out the best strategy to rob Joe, but all of the alcohol he'd consumed in his displeasure had him thinking wrong. Later, after he'd gotten her home, Cadillac continued getting wasted off of alcohol and blow.

"Baby, can you come rub some oil on my back?" Mist called to Cadillac as she entered their bedroom fresh out of the shower.

"Tell me you love me first," he demanded after grabbing her face and biting her cheek softly.

"I love you, daddy Caddie." She moved his hand away and kissed it. Seeing he was past his limit, she took his drink and finished it off for him. "Come on, daddy, do my back."

His hands slid down her back to her butt, then back up to her bare shoulders, spreading the silky oil over her soft, smooth skin. Mist had a body that made most woman jealous and every man want to explore it. But tonight, it was her man she'd made jealous. He suddenly began whacking her on the butt hard. Mist pulled away in pain from his repeated blows. He pulled her back to him.

"Come back here, bitch!" he barked, holding her in place, and roughly sucked on her breast.

She was tired and not in the mood for anything really besides sleep, but she didn't want to deny him, especially not in his state of mind. Her eyes closed as she let a moan escape her lips. The pleasurable sounds only brought pictures of Joe and his guys to Cadillac's mind. He violently shoved her away.

"What's wrong? Daddy, what did I do?"

"Bitch! Bitch, you think that hoe fag-ass nigga better than me, hoe!" he growled, then threw her to the floor.

Mist hit her mouth on the bed rail. Tasting her own blood, she scrambled to her feet. "Bae, you drunk. I don't know who or what you're talking about." She turned to go look at her lip, and he grabbed hold of her arm. Mist instantly slapped him as hard as she could.

"Bitch, you bad now? Tell me, is you bad? You want to fight me, bitch! That hoe-ass nigga can't save you up in my shit!" he yelled then slapped her back. "You, my bitch!" he exclaimed, grabbing her throat and squeezing.

Mist started kicking him, and her knee caught him in the groin. That blow only made him let go of her throat and hit her with a left and then a right fist that dropped her. Thinking fast, she reached into her bag lying on the floor next to where she fell, pulled out her blade, and slashed his hand and forearm when he moved to hit her again. Then she kicked him with all she had, then ran and locked herself in the bathroom. Immediately she dialed 9-1-1.

"Nine one one, what's your emergency?" the first responder answered.

"My boyfriend is drunk and fighting me. Send the police, please!"

"Where are you now, ma'am?"

"I'm locked in the bathroom."

"Did he lock you in the bathroom?"

"No, I did, to get away from him so I could call you."

"Where is he now? Is he still in the house?" The question was answered by Cadillac kicking on the door. "Ma'am? Ma'am, stay on the line. I'm sending help right now," the 911 operator said to a dead line.

Officers Hermit and Barr got to the call first. At the door they heard a female scream for help and kicked in the door, rushing to her aid. They found them fighting in the bedroom.

"Police, stop!" Hermit demanded.

"Fuck you, bitch! Get out my house," Cadillac shouted at the officers, then raised his hand to hit Mist again.

Without hesitation Officer Barr shot him with his taser. Cadillac promptly hit the floor hard and then placed him in handcuffs within seconds.

After he was taken to jail, Mist called me over, and the two of us packed up all her things and a few of his. She made sure we took all the two hundred-plus pounds of weed he'd just purchased, that had been fronted to him by his Chicago-based plug. Then she moved in with me. Mist started selling sacks of weed to the girls and a few guys at the club, until someone told the owner. The owner ordered a search of her locker, but she had sold out just as he did so. That close call was what made her talk me into taking it to the streets.

My big brother Monk is doing time up state in Waupun Correctional Institution for felony murder. Three years before he'd gotten caught up in a robbery while tryna conduct a drug deal. On a visit I told Monk about the large amount of weed and asked him could he help us get rid of it. A few days later he wrote me a letter with D-Man's name and number that he'd gotten from his cell mate. Monk charged us $100 and a few sexy pictures of Mist for the info.

D-Man spent $2,000 for a pound the first day we met up with him. I hit my brother with an additional $300. That had been over two months ago.

~ ~ ~

"Lac? Lac? Nigga, wussup, what's on yo mind?" Tuffy, one of his young goons asked, trying to pass Cadillac his drink.

"You niggas ready to get some money tonight? Our money train just pulled in."

"Always. I stay ready so I won't have to get ready. Getting ready might make me miss that payday. Ya feel me?" answered RedBoy, another of his goons.

"Alright, my nigga. Well that's my old bitch we been lookin' for and over there at VIP. Them the niggas we gonna tear off."

"Two for one, I'm always down with that," Tuffy replied, tipping one of the girls $2 as she passed their table.

Seeing Mist get off stage and walk straight over to Joe's booth in VIP made all Cadillac's remorseful thoughts from doing Mist wrong disappear and be replaced by ones of jealousy. A little over an hour later, him and his men sat outside of the car dealership where they'd followed their prey for the night. Money was on the minds of the young men, and deadly revenge was dancing in the mind of Cadillac.

ten

A BUSY FLIGHT FOR Life helicopter was being swarmed by medical staff after landing on top of St. Mary's hospital. This is where many of the victims of the Lake Michigan crash were being taken. The hospital's crisis response medical team rushed Peb through its Emergency Room with over 85 percent of her body badly burned. She had been standing on the deck smoking and talking with friends from her workout class when the collision happened. Peb was thrown from the ship through the flames before she came crashing down into the dark waters. Now doctors worked hard to save her life.

~ ~ ~

When I made it to the lake front docks, I immediately saw that police and the National Guard were hard at work in every direction I looked. I pushed my way through the crowds until I found Ariana talking to an officer.

"Where are they taking people from the crash?" I demanded. The officer that Ari was talking to made a call right away to get me the info I needed.

"Most are being taken to St. Mary's hospital, but there's really no way for me at this time to tell you if your family members have been taken there or any one of the other nearby hospitals," the officer explained.

"Okay, alright, thanks! Is she okay to go now?"

"Yes, I have all I need. I pray your friends or family are well!"

"Thank you! Come on, Ari, let's get to the hospital and see if they've been brought in yet. If not, the hospital should be able to help us more than anyone here." I noticed that she was still crying and shaking too hard to drive. So we got in my car. "We got to pray and hope for the best," I tried to console her, with tears of fear filling the wells of my eyes.

The large hospital was packed with family, friends, and reporters trying to get a word from whoever would speak to them. I gave my name and the names of my girls to the tense-looking nurse at the reception desk. "Just a minute." She picked up the phone. Moments later a nurse came and walked us to a room in the ICU wing. A doctor met us there.

"Mr. Lee, I don't want to stress her too much, so I'm going to allow you to go in and see her, but only for ten minutes. Afterward you and I can talk."

"Okay, that will be fine. Do you know if my wife Khadija Lee was brought in here too?"

"Not right off hand. I'll have someone look into it for you."

I turned to Ari. "You going to be alright?" She shook her head yes. "Will you two please go try an' find Dija for me?"

"Duda, I got Ari. We will find your wife if she's here. You just go see about Pebbles right now," Queen said moments before the heart monitor's alarm began screaming, alerting the response team to a flat-lining patient. The doctors and nurses rushed into Peb's room, pushing us out of the way. Before I could push my way into the room with them, the hospital security officers rushed me. They took my arm and hauled my ass off toward the family waiting area. Once in the room, I called Toochie while aggressively pacing the room.

"Man, fam, you must've read my mind. I was about to call you. I got some bad shit to lay on you, but I'm talking to the police right now," he told me when he answered the phone.

"Man, fuck what they talkin' 'bout! Tell 'em that you need to get here with Classy!" I barked at him.

"Get where? What's wrong?"

"What you mean what's wrong? I thought you was talkin' to the police. They didn't fuckin' tell you?" I snapped.

"Hold up, tell me what? I'm the one called 'em here because we got robbed, and Joe and Badd was killed in it."

"What the fuck!"

"What's wrong with Classy?" His voice was filled with worry now.

"The party boat crashed and blew up with everyone on it."

"What!" he screamed cutting me off.

"So far only Peb and Classy were found. The doctors are workin' on 'em now. I ain't heard shit on Khadija yet. I don't even know where she's at. But they're still bringin' in people."

"Oh God, man, fuck! This shit ain't happening!"

"Ari just went to see if they brought her in yet. We're at St. Mary's. Tell 'em you gotta get here now."

"I'm on my way." With that, we ended the call.

~ ~ ~

"What the fuck them fool-ass niggas do?" Cadillac asked himself aloud while watching Mist and Toochie fleeing the scene. He waited five minutes, then pulled out, calling Tuffy's cell. When he didn't answer, he called RedBoy and still received no answer. Cadillac knew then that his guys didn't make it. He shook his head as he rounded the block with the hope of being wrong. When he passed the car dealership the second time, the police were pulling up, so he drove up a ways and parked to observe the scene unfold.

More flashing lights hit the block, and he got low in the seat, trying his best to avoid being seen. He had to adjust the rearview mirror so he could see what was going on behind him. Cadillac watched the police walk RedBoy out in cuffs to an awaiting ambulance just as one was racing off in the direction of the nearest hospital.

A Channel 58 News van suddenly took its place. Cadillac knew at that point there was nothing he could do to help the guys. He wondered what had gone wrong as he rushed home to catch the breaking news report.

~ ~ ~

"They took your friend to the county hospital. Your car has to stay here, so you can ride with me or them. But I gotta go right the fuck now. My BM was in a bad accident."

"I'll ride with you. I don't got time for these muthafuckas nagging me an shit all the way to my house about what happen." Mist pulled out a blunt and started rolling it. "Can I use your phone to call my roommate? I left mine my car."

Toochie passed her his phone and then skillfully dodged a car that darted out in front of them.

"Hello?" I didn't know the number, but it had to be important to be calling me this late.

"Gurl, where you at? I need you to come get me from the county hospital."

"We're goin' to St. Mary's, not the county," Toochie corrected her.

"Oh. Okay. I mean St. Mary's hospital," she said, noticing the direction they were going.

"I'm already here at St. Mary's. Why you coming here?"

"You're where?"

"At St. Mary's. I'm here with Duda. The party boat crashed, and his people were brought here. What's going on with you?"

"I don't think I should say over the phone. But I'm okay. The new girl I took with me to do that show got shot. But I'm on my way there because my guy's baby mama was in an accident and brought there. What do you know about the crash 'cause ya know a lot of the girls from the club was on it?"

"I hope she wasn't on the boat," I said. "Let's just talk when you get here."

"Was your baby mama on that party boat?"

"Yeah. Who that you talkin' to?" Toochie questioned.

"My roommate. She's at the hospital. She went on that boat too?"

"I wasn't on the boat. Where's your phone? Never mind, I'll see you when you get here." I got off the phone with Mist and stopped and got a large hot cocoa for myself and two large coffees for Duda and Ariana. "Here you go. Drink this." I handed one to each of them.

"I don't drink coffee, but thanks anyway."

"I didn't know. You want my cocoa?"

"No, go head, I'm good."

"No, you can have the rest. I'm just going to mix a little with this coffee." He accepted it from me once I was done mixing the two drinks. I could see it relaxing him a bit. At least he sat down from all his pacing.

I didn't know what to do. I wanted to hold him, but told myself that would be the wrong thing to do at a time like this. I wondered what Mist had got herself into. I couldn't wait for her to get here so I could have a reason to get away. I closed my eyes and silently prayed for Duda's people and everyoneelse on the boat.

~ ~ ~

"How they doing, D? These people wouldn't tell me shit. They just put us in here an shit!" Toochie said when he walked into the family waiting area where we were.

"I ain't heard shit yet." I looked over his shoulder at the woman he had brought with him.

"Gurl, this who you with?" Queen asked, shocked to see the woman Toochie had walked in with.

"You two know each other?" I asked, knowing Mist from seeing her a few times at the club.

"Yes, this who I was waiting on," Queen explained. We passed the time by talking about what had happened with Toochie and Mist at the dealership.

Hours later the doctor and a few nurses walked into the waiting area and gave us the news. Neither one made it. Pebbles died in the recovery room, and Classy slipped away before she made it to the hospital.

I asked them if Khadija had been brought in yet. The doctor sent one of the nurses off to find out. She returned moments later and told us no, and we went home.

eleven

IS IT SWEET?

SINCE THE LOSS OF his goons, Cadillac had to
fall back and regroup. He easily recruited himself
some young cutthroats. DC, Rich, Moon, and Banks
made up the lieutenants of his bigger, more
dangerous clique. With them, he took over and
locked down Thirty-Third and Auer Avenue.
Cadillac had his hardheads in the hood hustling
hard, moving smack, blow, and kush in the streets
like hoes on the strip. He even had a few of them
breaking bread with him, but none of it was enough
for him. Making Mist pay for his broken heart was
all that was on his mind.

The night of the foiled robbery, he went back to
the dealership after the police, and everyone had
cleared out and found the 343 pounds of kush and
twelve bricks of heroin stashed in a shed. During his
reconnaissance the weeks before the robbery,
Cadillac observed Joe take known a few known
dealers in the shed empty-handed and leave with
bags. It had always been his target. His plan was to
send his goon inside to keep Joe and his guys busy
while he cleaned out the shed. Anything that he got
off them, he planned on splitting amongst his guys,

but nothing from what he took. Cadillac had one thing in his way of success, and that was Mist. He wanted her dead. But not more than he wanted her back.

After a week of hard grinding, he paid back his people for the weed that he lost when Mist had him locked up for that domestic violence charge. His connect hit him off with more plus a few pounds of pills. One looking to party could get it all in his hood. Just the way he wanted it. His only thing was he didn't know anybody who would mess with him with the kind of weight he needed in heroin. He needed to go down to Chicago and shop around for a connect.

"Hey, hey, Lac, I got somethin' up I think might be sweet down on the East."

"Like what?"

"My bitch sister fuckin' with this nigga on that end and say he holdin'."

"So how ya know she know what she's talkin' about?" Cadillac asked while snorting a line of blow.

"My bitch said today when she dropped her off, she went in to use the bathroom and the nigga had stacks of money just out on the table. She said her sister always tell her it just be the two of them at that house most of the time," Rich explained, dropping off the money his spot owed from the night before and that morning.

"We need that so I can go bust this move down in the city a lil earlier. Cuzo bitch ass said fam on Sixty-Fifth in the city got that shit for the low." He pointed to Banks, who was asleep in the La-Z-Boy chair. "So you two go down there and see what you can, and we going in that bitch."

"Today?" Rich questioned.

Cadillac took a second to think and said, "Why the fuck not?"

~ ~ ~

"Bitch, hurry the fuck up!" Cadillac snapped.

"Daddy, I only got two more ATMs to hit, and I'm done with these cards."

"Bitch, I hope so."

"I hate when you get like this, bae." Belle spoke in her Bluetooth as she walked away from the ATM's booth, checking the crowd. Nobody seemed to be interested in her. Then a black-and-white cop car hit the corner with only its lights on. She hurried to the car, and they pulled off into the heavy traffic.

The police didn't stop at the bank. They shot right past them in a hurry to get somewhere. "Bitch, what your heart beatin' for? You thought they was comin' fo' yo lil ass, didn't you?"

"So. Daddy Caddy let's get Burger King." Bella pointed to the one coming just up ahead. Cadillac's cell rang.

"Wussup, Killa, tell me you got somethin' good for me."

"I just holla at my nigga down the way. He got what you need right here in the Mil. His numbers right, too, for it to be here," Killa Rob told Cadillac as he whipped his rental lane to lane.

"Sounds good. Are we going to be able to do this before you head out to ATL?"

"I'm already gone. But he told me since I fuck with you to give you his number, and he will meet up with you. Bitch-ass nigga don't fuck this up on no hot shit! He only fuckin' with you because of me!"

"It's good. I got you, my nigga. As bad as I need this, I'd be a fool to fuck it up."

Killa Rob gave him the number, and Cadillac called and got it set up for later with D-Man. He was so glad to have the connect right here in the city, he pulled off without Bella and their food. "Oh shit!" He laughed as he turned to go back for her.

twelve

BROKENHEARTED

THE LAKE MICHIGAN CRASH was all over the news and papers. So, nobody paid it no mind when the News 6 report talked about the woman found in front of the art museum. Her report said the Jane Doe was taken to the county hospital.

My mother came and took the boys off my hands, but Coco refused to leave me alone. Babygirl only broke down once in front of her little brothers. She was doing her best to be strong for all of us. All I could do was let her do her. I was a mess myself.

I took care of Peb's funeral arrangements and got myself prepared for a custody battle over my boys with their grandparents, especially since only one of them was mine. I wasn't going to let them split them up, and we never knew or cared who Trayvon's father was. I loved him from the first time I met him, and that'd been it.

To my surprise, all Peb's parents made me do was promise not to keep them away from none of the kids. My mother did one better and took turns with them helping me with the boys. I was reduced to being a weekend dad with my sons.

Toochie wasn't so lucky with his children. Classy's parents took them from him after he showed up to the funeral late and drunk.

We were both taking our losses hard. I believe mine was a bit harder because I didn't have Dija body to say goodbye to, and I wasn't ready to give up on finding it.

~ ~ ~

"Daddy, Grandpa say you got to get your act together before we can live back at home with you. When you going to be done with your act? I miss my house and all my stuff, and you, too, Dad."

Toochie eye's watered. "Son, Daddy misses you and loves you and your sisters very much. I'm going to work hard to get it together so I can bring you back home. How would you like if I came up there and spent the day with you?"

"Yeah! That will be good! Can we go to the movies and to eat pizza like we use to do before Mama had to go with God?"

"We can do whatever you want." After the call with his kids, Toochie sat in front of his marble gas fireplace looking at a family photo, drinking. His kid's words replaying over and over in his mind. He decided right then and there he was done feeling sorry for himself. He downed the last of his drink and then walked out the door. He was sure his sons seen right though the phony tough-guy front he put on.

The loss of Classy had weakened him. He had all the money and the power now that Joe was gone. But he didn't have his family to share it with. He wondered if he would ever find a woman worthy of being a part of his kids' life to start over with.

He didn't know how long he had been walking when his cell phone rang, breaking him from his thoughts. "What?" he answered without looking at it.

"What? Where are you? You got this door open. I thought something was wrong," Ariana said, putting down her gun and walking back to the front door.

"I. I. went for a walk to clear my head."

"Where are you? Let me come get you?" she begged, not liking the tone of his voice.

"I'm just down the street. I'm on my way right back home."

Ari was waiting at the door as he came down the street. When he saw the worry in her face, he knew she felt something for him and felt bad for making her worry. She took his hand, and he followed her into the house. When he looked down into her eyes she could see the hurt and loneliness in his. His lips parted to say something, but she cut him off with hers. Ari didn't know what she could do to help him to ease his broken heart. She knew tonight, this moment, she would not deny him any part of her.

He broke the kiss and stepped closer into her arms, feeling like he belonged there. His tears fell freely for his friend and wife. She held him there in her arms until the tears stopped and she felt his hot mouth on her neck tracing the path his tears made. Soon they were naked on the floor in front of the fireplace. She was the woman he had been with since Classy's death. Every thought of him and his wife flashed before him the deeper and deeper he stabbed into Ariana's warmth.

thirteen

BAD TIMING

DODGING MEN CARRYING HEAVY steel beams, I found a safe place to stand as I spoke on the phone.

"My nigga, be on your shit. I'll be at the shop for the rest of the day. So, when you ready for me, I'm ready," I said to D-Man while watching the workers install the car lift.

"I'll be good, my nigga. Killa Rob won't send nobody my way on no bullshit. He know I get down fo' real fo' real, but it ain't gonna come to that."

"Let's hope not. Who down there with you right now?"

"I'm good, my nigga. Josh just walked in with the dawg food you sent."

"Alright, just hit me. I gotta see what these fools doin' in the back." I hung up with the feeling something bad was going to happen. When one of the workers fell from the car lift, breaking his arm, I figured that was the reason for my feeling. So, I pushed the negative thoughts about deal my folks was about to do out of my mind.

~ ~ ~

Moon picked up Cadillac in a rental and headed down to the address D-Man gave them. Before they stopped in front of the address, Cadillac called to let D-Man know he was outside. "Come on up. I see you in the black Ford, right?"

"Yeah, that's us," Cadillac answered. Moon put on his gloves and checked his gun. Cadillac grabbed the money off the backseat, and they went into the house. Nobody noticed the three men in the car parked just off the opposite corner from the house.

In the car were Rich Banks and Man-Man. When they saw they boss go into the house with Moon, they decided it would be a good time to run up in there, not thinking of how Cadillac knew the house or person they were just told about earlier that day.

~ ~ ~

In the house, Moon noticed it was two females who D-Man sent away into one of the bedrooms. He also noticed Josh, who proudly showed off his two Glock 23s.

Cadillac saw everything was set up for them on a large dining room table. None of this made him

wonder or sparked his memory of what Rich had
told him, because he was too high at the time.

"Y'all want something to drink or something
while I count slow?" D-Man joked.

"Take your time. But can I see the work while
you counting? Like to see what I'm buying before I
make a commitment."

"I'll take one of the Red Bulls," Moon spoke up.

Josh passed him the drink and for the first time
noticed Moon's hands were covered. He just smiled
at the young shooter. "You smoke?" he asked
Moon.

"For sho. I was just thinking 'bout the B I got in
the ashtray. Straight up."

~ ~ ~

Rich drove to the gas station on Holton and
bought three white tees to use to mask their faces.
Once they found a good place to park in back of an
abandoned house, they put the shirts over their
heads and tied them around their faces before
walking up to the house.

"You stay here and look out," Banks instructed
Man-Man.

"Alright, I'll be on the side of the house."

"Cool cool. You ready to do this, my nigga?"

"Born ready," Rich answered.

With a plan set, Rich and Banks got out of the car and then hit the same door they seen Cadillac walk into. Josh jerked his head toward the door when he heard the footsteps. So did Moon, who was sitting close to the door. When the door burst open, Moon swiftly pulled his 9mm and shot toward the door while ducking out the way.

Rich and Banks returned fire, just missing Josh, who dove to the right. Cadillac looked at the door, then back to D-Man, and pulled his .375 Mag.

"Come on!" D-Man called to him, immediately running toward the kitchen. Cadillac followed him, running to keep up.

"What the fuck up, fam?" Cadillac's finger tightened on the trigger once he and D-Man were in the back hallway.

"Fuck, I don't know! I almost thought this was you," he responded, holding his .44 Mag down to show Cadillac he didn't mean him any harm.

"Let's get the fuck out of here and talk the rest later."

D-Man opened the back door and was met face-to-face with the master Man-Man. The youngster hesitated, seeing his boss, and D-Man blew his brains all over the house next door.

~ ~ ~

Back in the house, the shootout still raged on. "Moon, stop shooting at us!" demanded Rich.

"What the fuck you niggas doin'?" he asked, surprised it was one of his own.

Before he could get his answer, Josh shot him three times easily from where he was. "You bitch-ass niggas! It ain't sweet! It ain't sweet!" He jumped up, firing both guns as he crashed through the same door the two females went in earlier.

Rich was hit in the arm and ran back to the front door. But Banks went on for what they came for. He ran toward the dining room, thinking to himself how he would deal with Rich later.

As he gathered the money and dope. Josh opened the door and stepped out slowly. Banks heard him and met him with a shot to the side of Josh's head. Thinking it was over, he turned to get the dope and money. That's when Bree shot him in the back with Josh's other gun he gave her when he got in the room.

Bree didn't stop pulling the trigger until she seen him fall. Then her and Anna grabbed all the and ran out the door, where they were met by more of D-Man goons who took them across the street to the safe house.

~ ~ ~

A police car in the area responding to the shot spotter cut D-Man and Cadillac off as they exited the alley. They both fired at the police car and then raced away, splitting up. D-Man cut through a few yards heading to another of the hood's safe houses.

Cadillac ran back toward the house he'd come from. He smartly cut through the yard of the house next door and was surprisingly met by a guy with a gun. Without hesitation Cadillac shot him point-blank in the face and kept going. Another one of D-Man's goons seen this and turned his gun on Cadillac, promptly sending shots his way from an angry AK-47.

At the sound of the big gun, Rich looked up from his hiding place in the car. He couldn't see the shooter, but he could see his boss was the one being shot at. He started the car and spun it around, heading to pick up Cadillac. Rich brought the car to a hard stop, then aimed his gun out the window and sent shots toward the shooter with the AK.

"Lac? Lac? Come on! Lac?" he yelled, calling Cadillac to the car as he frantically pulled the trigger.

Cadillac, not being able to hear Rich summoning him because of all of the loud gunfire shots, took the open opportunity caused by Rich and the shooters' exchange to make a run for the rental. He knew Moon had left the keys on the floor just in case they got into trouble.

Seeing Cadillac run past him, Rich stormed off, but another man with a 12-gauge sent shots his way. One of the shots just missed his head, blowing out the driver-side back window. Rich whipped the car around the corner, not bothering to slow down and suddenly ramming a responding police SUV. The impact from the speeding vehicle sent the police car flipping over onto its side. Bloody and dazed, Rich clawed his way out of the wreckage, still attempting to make his escape.

fourteen

SLOW DOWN

"I AIN'T SEEN OR heard shit from that nigga Lac since I had lil bro take him them books he came for."

"Thought you said the money was light?"

"It is. I believe that it's on my end, not his. Bitches been shopping good around this muthafucka an shit. It ain't shit though! I just want to know who ran up in my shit!"

"Keys said one of them niggas name Man-Man, an' he off the trays. I would say it was the nigga Lac's doin', but you said them niggas was at his head too. This shit crazy."

"Yeah, the police fucking with me because I don't have a lease for the person I rented the place out to. I gotta take them hoes something with the renter's name on it, or they gon' try to put all that shit on me."

"I'll have Tywannie handle that for you. I'ma text her right now and have her put the house in Josh name. Is that okay?"

"I don't give a fuck. I just don't want 'em to take my house," D-Man said just as the waitress brought us our food. "You wanna wait on the girls?"

"Don't got to. Here they come now," Duda announced, glancing up from the message he was texting.

"Before you put it down, tell your bitch she can come join us if she can't wait to see you, because I'm not letting you get away from me tonight," I said, taking my seat next to Duda.

"That's what the fuck I'm talkin' 'bout, my nigga!"

"What the fuck ever, D-Man. Try and bring another bitch in our bed if you want," Bree warned him.

~ ~ ~

"Caddy, did you like my dance?" asked the tall, slim redbone dancer bypassing the rest of the men at the table who tipped and felt on her tight ass as she passed.

"You know how I do, bitch. I want to see if you can do all that tricky shit on this dick."

"It ain't hard for you to find out." She put on her best smile. "Can I have a tip?"

"Bitch, tip your fool ass out my daddy face unless you trying to be down and break bread, bitch!" Sony snapped, coming up from behind the girl and sitting in Cadillac's lap.

"I guess you got a choice to make, hoe. Leave now or break bread, bitch." Cadillac said, downing his shot of Patrón. The girl rolled her eyes at Sony and walked off. Cadillac's eyes followed her small, tight butt until they landed on the next dancer taking the stage.

She was the girl of his nightmares. He always loved the way Mist worked the pole. Sony seen who he was looking at. "Do you want her, daddy? I know that bitch want me because she asked me to do a girl-on-girl with her once," she lied. Sony and Mist had never said a real word to one another the entire time they'd been working at the club together.

"I know her already. We're old friends, but if you can get her to bring the bitch to the room so I can see what she on first." He imagined being between Mist's legs again and felt himself start to become erect.

~ ~ ~

The sound of the shower woke me up. I had to let my eyes get use to the strange darkness. I'm use to the morning sun pouring in through my bedroom windows. Instinctively I reached for the lamp and found it wasn't there. It was in that moment I realized where I was—that and the sweet pains that shot through my body from the workout Duda put on me hours before.

I sat up on the edge of the bed, then quietly made my way into the bedroom with him. Seeing his silhouette through the frosted steamy shower glass made my kitty purr. Right then I decided I was going to get in another round.

When I opened the door and he seen me standing there still naked, he didn't have to say a word, and I didn't let him. I stepped in, knelt down, grabbed his semihard length, and took all of him in my mouth. I sucked him, licking the head of his now-hard shaft like it'd been mine for years. Then I swallowed him deep into my throat, making him grow harder and bigger. I backed off to catch my breath but continued to lick and suck on his tip while at the same time working one hand up and down his shaft and playing with his balls with the other. Soon I felt it jerk between my lips and knew he was close to cumming. Duda then took over. He pushed me away, spun me around, and thrust himself into my wetness, hard and fast from behind. I had to brace myself with my hands against the wall to keep him from banging my head on it.

He was hitting it just right, nice and hard, until I felt his hardness spasm inside me, throwing me over the edge into a wild orgasm. Duda didn't stop his stride; he just keep fucking me. I couldn't believe he was still going strong after busting in me. Oh God, this man didn't know what he was doing to me. "I love you!" Fuck! I shouldn't have said that out loud. He still didn't stop or skip a beat, so maybe he didn't hear me. "I love you fuckin' me like this! Get this pussy, babe! Get it!" I shouted, hoping to cover my slip of tongue.

~ ~ ~

"Bitch, where you at, hoe?"

"I'm with daddy tramp having a late breakfast, so make it quick," I told Mist, glancing over the table at Duda playing a game on is iPad while I talked on the phone.

"I was with Lac last night," Mist said, excited.

"Lac? Cadillac? Bitch, is you crazy! After what went on with him and you—hell, with us—and you fuckin' with that bitch again?"

"I didn't know he was the person I was going to do the show for when I went, but it was cool. He wasn't mad at me or on nothing crazy. I don't even think he knows we took his stuff. All he kept telling me was how much he misses me and still has feelings for me."

I could hear the excitement in her voice but couldn't believe it. I knew I needed to make her slow her roll with him. "Bitch, have you lost your damn mind? I'm not going to get in this with you right now. I'll call you when I'm on my way to the house, so don't get caught up in shit until we talk."

"See, you trippin', but okay. I gotta go get my nails fixed for work tonight right quick. After that I'm going straight home to take my punk ass to sleep."

"Whuteva, just know this conversation ain't over." I ended my call with her just as Duda's cell rang. I took over his game while he spoke with his daughter. I knew it was her from her ringtone and the photo that popped up of her when she called.

"What's wrong?" I heard him ask her. I stopped playing, hearing the seriousness in his voice. "Come on, we gotta go right now!" he ordered me while still on the phone with his daughter. He looked like he had seen a ghost. I didn't protest; I just followed him out the door.

"Baby, what's wrong? Is Coco okay?" I asked, slightly jogging to keep up with him on the way to his car.

"I don't know. I mean, she okay. It's." His words trailed off and we got in the car.

fifteen

"HEY, BOO! WHAT YOU DOING?"

"Hey, you. I just sitting here talking to Nu Nu ass in front of her grandma house."

"Tell her I said what up. Can you do me a big favor?"

"It depends. What is it? I already know it has something to do with taking you somewhere, don't it?"

"Where that big-head bitch trying to go?" Nu Nu dipped in.

"Tell her to shut the hell up with her good hearing ass," Tashay said. laughing. "Girl, I need to go to the hospital. They just texted me the woman I've been taking care of all this time just woke up from her coma. I'm trying to be there to see if she remembers me reading her all the books and stuff for the past nine months."

"Boo Boo, you can keep it real with me. You just want to make sure you get that good report for school." Coco laughed. "I'll do it for you. I'm bringing Nu Nu wit me because this would be good for her to write about in the school paper."

"I don't care. Bring her slow ass."

"Nu Nu, grab your stuff and come on. You said you wanted me to help you think of something good to write about. You can't get no better than a woman waking up from a nine-month coma. So get your stuff so I can drop you with her," Coco said, pressing the remote start on her car.

After dropping them off, Coco didn't make it a full five blocks away when her cell phone started playing the tone set for Nu Nu. She thought she must've forgotten something in the car, so she pulled over as she answered to look in the backseat.

"What you forget?"

"Coco! Coco, you need to get back now, and call your daddy too."

"Why? What's wrong?" she asked, hearing the concern in Nu Nu's voice.

"This your mother Shay been taking care of. Get back here now!"

"Bitch, you know I don't play like that."

"No, I'm fo' real. I wouldn't play with you on something like this. It's her. Her hair is almost all gray and she's smaller, but it's her. Call your daddy and get back here."

Coco's heart pounded faster at the thought of it really being her mother. Her hands shook so hard she dropped her phone when I answered.

~ ~ ~

It was happing all over again. Queen and I made it to the hospital in one piece. I let her out in front of the entrance so I could have a few moments alone to collect myself as I looked for a parking spot. When I rejoined Queen, we entered together, and I gave my name to the nurse at the reception desk as well as stated the reason I was there. After putting all of the information in the computer, she picked up the phone, and a lazy uniformed guard came to the desk. "Norris, this is Mr. Lee," the nurse introduced with a smile. "Would you mind taking him back to the open coma ward? His wife is there."

"No problem. Would you follow me please?" He took us to the southwest elevator. Before we got to her floor, a nervousness shot through me I can't explain. I forced myself to step off of the elevator when it landed on her floor and to keep moving as we went down the hallway. My thoughts were racing like a hundred miles per second. I'd briefly forgotten that Queen was with me. When we turned the corner, I could make out the girls sitting huddled up outside of the room. I instantly took off in a slight jog over to my daughter and her friend, leaving the guard and Queen chasing behind me.

"Coco?" My Babygirl looked up as I came to a stop in front of her.

"Daddy, it's Mama! It's really her!" Tears of joy and exhaustion flowed from my little girl's eyes.

"Why y'all out here instead of in there with her? How is she?" I anxiously inquired.

"She had some breathing issues, chest pains. It got hard for her to breathe, so the doctors put us out until they got done getting her stabilized," Shay explained. "I'm sorry I didn't know. She just don't look herself to me. I'm really sorry."

"It's okay. I thank you for takin' care of her all this time. At least I know she was in caring hands."

"She don't remember nothing or nobody," Nu Nu blurted out, informing me of Khadija's memory loss.

"Not even me, Daddy. Not even me!" My Babygirl started crying harder.

"The doctors can't say if she will get her memory back," Shay explained.

The doctor came out of the room. "Are you, her husband?"

"Yes, I am. How is she? Can I see her?"

"She was in a bit of a shock, so I had to give her something to help her relax. She's sleeping now, but I'll give you five minutes. Just don't wake her please." He told me after he looked into the room again himself.

"Come here, Coco. You should let your dad do this alone." Queen tried to comfort Coco when I vanished into the room.

Khadija was very thin and pale, but it was my wife. It was really her. Tears slipped from my eyes as I stood there looking at my beautiful wife. I don't know how long I just stood there staring at her. I didn't hear the door open, or the footsteps come up behind me.

"Sir, you're going to have to go now. You can come back this evening," the nurse told me.

"I'm her husband. Is her doctor still here?"

"Oooh, I'm sorry! I didn't know." She looked embarrassed. "I'll get the doctor for you, but could you please step out and wait for him?"

Reluctantly, I followed the surprised nurse out the door back into the hallway, where she called the doctor using a hanging microphone on the wall across from my wife's room.

sixteen

WHO YOU WITH?

I DROVE COCO'S CAR back and got my own. So many thoughts were rushing through my mind. I was happy and getting sadder by the minute. I was happy that Khadija is pretty much alright, and they had been reunited. But where did that leave us? He couldn't really look me in my face before I left. No kiss, no hug, just a promise to call me. When I made it into the house, Mist was walking out of the bathroom. "Hey!"

"Hey! What time do you gotta be at work tonight?" I asked, looking at my watch.

"Tonight? Seven thirty, But I'm up so early because I'm going to meet up with Lac. He takin' me."

"Lac is gonna to take you somewhere and kill yo dumb ass, girl! I told you not to do shit until we talked."

"We talkin' now, and I'm tellin' you I'm good. I know how to handle him. You look like you been crying. Wuddup with you?" Mist asked, still dressing.

"Something flared my allergies," I lied. "You didn't have that fool up in here or tell him where we live, did you?" I put the subject back on her.

"No, Mother, I didn't," she replied, being sarcastic. "I'm gonna meet up with him. I promise to be careful. I know who I'm dealing with, Cadillac, aka a fool with his head game. I'm just tryna to get that chocolate muthafucka between these thighs again, only without his little bitch around."

"What? What bitch?"

She told me the story about how they got back together and the threesome the nigga actually paid her for. Either he was up to something, or he really did miss her. Sooner or later, he was going to want to know where his money was for the weed we took. I told her this over and over until it was time for her to go meet up with him.

I called in to work. I just didn't feel up to it. I ran me a hot bath filled with jasmine oil, filled me a big glass of wine, drank, half refilled it, rolled a joint, and played with my memories of Duda and I in the shower just that morning.

~ ~ ~

Mist made her way through the packed sports bar. She took a seat and waved to the bartender, an old friend who knew what she wanted. She looked around for Cadillac but didn't see him or anyone else she knew. When she felt a hand on her shoulder, she turned. "What you drinkin'?"

"Wildberry Cuervo."

"I just got this one. You can pay for it since you buyin'." She smiled. "I'm surprised you even noticed me with my clothes on."

"All that. How long have we known each other? Some might think we fuckin' around or some shit. Are you here by yo'self?" Toochie asked after telling the bartender to put her drink on his table's tab.

"For right now I am. I'm waiting on someone to meet me here."

"You can wait with us if you want." He pointed at a table with two other men sitting looking at a game.

"I gotta pass on that offer. It won't be a good look for me with the guy I'm meetin'."

"What wouldn't be a good look?" Cadillac asked from behind them.

"Hey, Boo! How long you been here?" Mist stood up to face him, heart racing a bit.

"Not long. Who this?" he asked knowing good and well who Toochie was.

"It's good, fam, I ain't tryna step on your toes. Mist, give me a call, and we can see what we can do about gettin' you in that new car."

Mist accepted one of Toochie's cards and told him she would call, letting him know she caught on. What she didn't know was Cadillac had seen them leave the club together more than once before.

"How long you been waitin' on me?" Cadillac asked.

"Not long, this my first drink," she answered, looking at him watching Toochie walk back to his seat.

"Did you eat yet? We can order."

"No, but I don't want to eat here. It's too much like bein' at work. Let me finish my drink and we can go."

Cadillac ordered a shot of Patrón and a beer. They talked about the threesome. Mist drilled him about the girl. She had plans on sitting her down when she got to work to milk her for information about Cadillac. He openly told her things and

answered her questions. When they were done with
their drinks, they walked back to his old-school
1990 Cadillac DeVille, midnight blue, white,
and gold.

"I didn't know if you was comin' fo' real or
not," he admitted, opening the car door for her, then
going around and getting n behind the wheel. Mist
didn't talk. She just watched him as he drove,
thinking about how he kept looking back at Toochie
and wondering what was going on in his mind. The
talk she had with me had her on point. "Where do
you want to go eat?" He could see her looking at
him out of the corner of his eye.

"Did you ask to see me again because
you hungry?"

He pulled in and parked in a shady corner of the
nearest parking lot. The windows were dark,
making it hard to see inside. He looked at her, "No,
but I can see what I have a taste for. "He leaned
toward her and made her seat fall back. Then he
pulled her dress up to find her panties.

He started kissing her down low. She pulled his
head toward her as his warm tongue worked her clit,
sending tiny shockwaves through her body. She
reached down in his pants to free him and found his

manhood not hard but not soft either. Mist wrapped her hand around his length and gently squeezed on it. With a few strokes of her hand, Mist felt him warm and stiffen in her fist. She shuddered with excitement as she straddled Cadillac's lap and guided his hardness into her wet warmth. She rode him vigorously, rocking back and forth on him and cumming on him as she took him deeper and deeper into her warmth. Suddenly she started convulsing, and in one fluid motion Cadillac rolled her over, pushed her legs wide, and rammed his thick length in her hard and fast. Mist did her best to match Cadillac's passion with every stroke, but he knew just how she liked to be fucked, so in no time she was having a full orgasm right there on his seat. After cumming together, they found the nearest motel and checked in for round two. Afterward they took a shower together. It was almost time for Mist to go to work.

"Tell me you love me now like you did when you were riding this eight and a half incher, if you meant it." He laughed.

"Ha! You funny. Boo, you know I still got feelin's fo' you. I wouldn't be here if I didn't," she admitted as she stood in the mirror trying to do her best to untangle her long, kinky-twist braids.

"Do you got enough feelin's to help me out with somethin'?"

This is it, she thought. "Something like what?"

"I'm trying to hit that nigga you were talking to in BW3s."

"I don't know him like that. All I know is he sell cars," she lied. Cadillac didn't want her to know he had anything to do with her friend getting shot almost a year ago. "Ain't none of that stopped you before. I just need you to get him someplace and call me. I'll do the rest. Don't act like you don't remember how we use to do it, Mist."

"I don't know if I wanna be a part of that shit. It don't look like you hurtin' for cash anyway, Lac, so why do you wanna do it? Is it because you seen me talkin' to him?" With that inquiry, she seen his nose flare, which was a telltale sign of him getting angry, so she quickly changed the subject. "Boo, I gotta get back to my car so I can go to work. I'll think about it if you got a better plan than what you just said," Mist attempted to bargain as she thought about what I'd said about him taking her somewhere to kill her. She moved closer to her bag, where she had a pretty pink 25-caliber handgun hidden for times like these.

"Okay, I'll let you know when I come up with one, but I'm not goin' back out, so call you a ride or don't go in tonight. Stay here with me," he told her, then laid down on the bed.

seventeen

BOSS WANTS YOU

Back at the sports bar, Toochie's cell phone began
vibrating on his waist. He seen that the call was
coming from me. Knowing what was going on with
Khadija, Toochie excused himself from his guys
and walked outside, away from the loud cheering
that almost everyone was doing for the Milwaukee
Bucks game playing on the TV screens surrounding
the bar. Once out front, he immediately returned my
missed call. "Talk to me, my nigga. What's good
with sis?"

"I don't want to jinx us by speakin' too soon, so
I'll let you know after the doctor get done doin'
what he do. But on another Santos called lookin' fo'
you, my nigga. Wussup with that?"

"Fuck, man! I don't got my other cell with me.
It's been on the charger at the house for the past two
days," he promptly explained. "What he talkin'
'bout though?"

"Shit, he said he got his plane waiting on one of
us right now. He don't care who; he just wants to
see one of us in person by tomorrow. The old man

knows about Dija," I told him, voicing my surprise. "He told me to let him know if it's anything he can do to help."

"Joe, may he rest in peace, always said that the old man was everywhere. But I'm with Blu and Lorenzo at BW3s watchin' the game. I'ma call Ari and ask her to run to my crib and bring me my phone so I can call him."

"Man, Toochie, don't get fucked up and forget to get up with him. I don't got time for no shit with 'em down there. Now I got Dija back, I'm seriously thinkin' 'bout being on my way to full retirement from this shit."

"All our numbers and shit have been right, so I don't know why he callin' us. I'ma go. I'm about to call the nigga as soon as I get my other line. I got this! You just worry about sis. I got this fo' real."

"Alright, fam. Let me know when you touch down there tomorrow."

"I got you." We got off the phone, and he called Ariana. Once she brought him his phone, he placed the call to Santos and was told that Mr. Santos only wanted to speak to him in person. "Shit, Ari, he want me down there fo' real."

"I know, Duda called me already. I packed you an overnight bag. It's outside in the car. I know your ass want to finish this game, so we don't have to rush to the airport."

"We?"

"Yeah, we, nigga. I'm goin' with you. I ain't tryna let you fuck with them Spanish hoes he got waiting on you touchdown down there. I know how y'all do."

"It ain't even like that, bae." He smiled.

"Tell me anything." She drank the rest of his drink while he ordered them another.

~ ~ ~

The storm made it hard for them to sleep on the flight. So Toochie passed time playing Call of Duty, and Ariana read the latest urban release by Assa Reigns. It was approximately four in the morning when they finally arrived to Santos's villa. The housekeeper showed them where they would be sleeping. Once in their room, Ariana walked over to the window and found that it looked out over almond trees blossoms, which was a somewhat special thing to see that far south of the southern border.

"This place is so pretty. It's like a movie."

"I'll ask him if we can get a tour around the place before we leave." He looked at the excitement in her eyes. "I'll ask him if we can stay a few extra days to fuck it!" Ariana had been nothing but there for him since Classy's death. He felt he owed her this much and more.

Around midafternoon they were awakened by a soft knock on the door. "Yes, just a minute," Ariana answered. "Bae? Bae!" she exclaimed as she shook Toochie awake. He got up, went to the door, and was told Mr. Santos requested to see him at two. then the young boy took their orders for brunch and disappeared back down the hall, leaving them to get dressed.

eighteen

THE MEET

AT 1:45 P.M., TOOCHIE FOLLOWED an armed
guard down the marble hall to a thick pine door,
where he knocked lightly. It opened, and the guard
waved for Toochie to enter, then closed it behind
him. "Mr. Toochie, please have a seat. Mr. Santos
will be a minute," said the long, reddish-brown-
haired Spanish woman who now stood in front of
him. He sat down. "If there's anything you need,
please let me know."

"Sure will." The office looked and smelled like
money. He seen some cigars. "Could I have one of
these?" He pointed.

"Sure." She went over to the humidor and got
him the cigar, a match, and a cutter, then returned to
her seat behind a desk in the far corner of the large
room.

"Thank you! What do you do here?"

"You're welcome. I'm Mr. Santos's personal
assistant. I do what I'm told." She smiled.

"Sounds like fun." He smoked. Soon he began
to wonder why he was there again. He did a mental

checklist, and all that came to mind was good and on point. He trusted me with his life, so he knew not to think ill of me. He would just have to wait until he was told.

The office was on a corner of the house. Two of the walls were made of clear glass windows. Through one he could see a huge, beautiful garden, and through the other, rows and rows of cotton waiting to be plucked.

Ten minutes later Mr. Santos walked in. He motioned for Toochie to take the seat across from him after they shook hands. "Toochie, it's good to see you. You've been a hard man to catch up with lately. My sympathy goes out to you and your children for the loss of your lovely wife."

"Thank you!" Toochie responded just as another one of Santos's armed guards walked another gentleman in the office. Toochie looked at both of them curiously but waited for one of them to speak first.

Mr. Santos opened by introducing the little man as one of Japan's biggest underbosses. Now he really wondered why he was there. "I know you're wondering why I asked you here on such short notice. So let's skip the bullshit and get to the point." Mr. Santos took a sip of his limed ice water, then continued, "You have issues with others taking over your blocks or hoods, as you may call them."

"What? I don't know who told you that bullshit, but it ain't true," Toochie defended.

"If it's not true, how is it that Meinecke, Wright, Clark, and Center are all buying from this street punk Cadillac?" Mr. Yang asked. "We never really had those areas. We may fuck with one or two folks from them parts, but they're not ours."

"Fuck that! That side of the city is ours," Mr. Santos snapped. "Everything that's being sold, big or small, we should have part of. And with you and Duda being my men, you should hold all of it. But you spend too much time drunk in fucking strip clubs to be watching my money."

"Hold up, no matter what I do on my time, the money's always on point. We haven't took no losses since Joe's death, and that was made up for times two." Toochie sat back in his chair. "And Lac shops with us through one of our guys on the Eastside. So he can't be an issue here," he said, and took a pull of his cigar. "So what's really good? Why am I here?"

"Okay, okay, but you're wrong about Lac, as you call him. He just closed a deal with Mr. Lor here, who has an agreement with me to split the city in half. He has the south and we the north. Now this Lac is on the north, isn't he?" He went on before Toochie could answer, "Also, we got word that it was his men found dead in that Eastside robbery. What do you have to say about that?"

Toochie thought for a second. What would Joe do right now? he asked himself before he answered. "I'll take care of it."

"That's what I wanted to hear. But what do we do about Mr. Lor's loss?"

"He ain't lost shit. You two have an agreement, and by him continuing to fuck with Lac, he ain't complying with that agreement." Toochie stood. "But because he came to us with this like the businessmen we are, I will move his and ours for one month. That's more than fair."

"Yes it is, and I believe we have a deal, Mr. Toochie," Lor said, shaking Toochie's hand.

nineteen

NO PLACE LIKE

"HOW ARE YOU FEELING this morning?" the doctor asked, looking over the clipboard he was studying.

"Good morning! I feel alright. I had that dream again about the woman, but this time it had Coco, the girl that you say is my daughter, and two little boys in it."

"Does it mean anything to you? Were there others in it like your husband or brother?" he asked, knowing some of her family background.

"No. I mean I don't remember. When I try, my head hurts." It was hard for her to believe that she was married and had a child. "In my dream me and this woman were partners, but I'm married. At least that's what everyone tells me," Khadija explained.

"Well maybe today it will make some sense to you. I'm releasing you to go home with your husband and daughter."

"Okay. okay, but what if. ? Do you think. ?" She couldn't find the words to express what she wanted to say.

"Don't worry. Family is always the best treatment for cases like yours. A nurse will be at your call at all times and will do daily home visits for the first week, then twice a week after that if all goes well." The doctor explained, trying to relax her a bit.

"Hey, beautiful, you ready to come home?" I asked when I entered the room. I was way past nervous, but I did my best to keep it hidden and went all out to make her homecoming as comfortable as possible. The nurse was his idea. Me and Coco bought the types of flowers she liked and placed them in each room, and we filled the house with things she liked to eat and loved to cook for us. I even drove her car when it was time to pick her up in. Whatever could be done, we did it.

Khadija's parents thought it would be best if I waited to bring the boys around. They didn't want to overload her or have her reject them, because they were too young to understand what was going on with their mother. It was hard enough explaining to them that she was back from heaven.

"Mama not going to try to eat us or suck out our brains, is she?" they had asked me. All I could do was laugh and hug my sons. I did my best to assure them she wouldn't and told myself I would talk to my father-in-law about what he watched with them on TV.

"Can I have some time to freshen up?" Khadija asked.

"I thought you would say that, so I brought you something to put on and a few personals I thought you might want."

A few hours after getting her home, Khadija moved around the house, unsure if she belonged there. Then little things started to come to her, like how she didn't like people eating in her living room and that she had bought paint so we could repaint the dining room and hallway. After about two hours of just sitting around the house, the girls asked her out shopping.

"Daddy, let me get your card so I can take Mama out with us."

"First, that's not how you ask me for things, and I'm not giving you and them bighead girls my card. I wouldn't let you set me up for that one. But here." I counted out $800 for them. "Make sure to take her to some stores she likes and keep a good eye on her. Call me if she remembers anything else, okay?"

"Okay, can I take my car, or do we got to take Mama's?"

"You can take yours if you want. I'm going to go by the auto shop to make sure them fools working and not sitting around getting me for my money."

Coco walked back into the living room all smiles. "He said we can go, and he gave me $800 to spend," she explained excitedly. "Ma, you still coming with us?"

"Are you sure you and your friends don't want to go by yourselves? I'll be alright if you do."

"No, we want you to come with us. It'll be fun!" Nu Nu spoke up.

"Okay." When they went outside, Dija said, "Let's take this car. It's mine, right?"

"Yeah, that's yours, but I know Daddy don't want me to drive your car."

"Who said you were driving?" Khadija smiled.

"Mama, are you sure you up to it?"

"Babygirl, get the keys and let's go." Dija walked around her A6, remembering when she first laid eyes on it. When Coco returned with the keys, she told her, "You handle the radio, and I'll do the driving. We going to Bay Shore, right?" she asked when they all got in the car.

"Yeah. Do you remember how to get there? Wait! You remembered the name of the mall we always go to!" Coco said excitedly.

"I did?" Khadija looked puzzled for a moment. "Now let's see if I know how to get there." Everything about the car and movement seemed right to her. The drive to the mall was smooth. When she found a parking spot, she sat there blinking back a flashback of the last time she was there with Peb. When they got out of the car, she held Coco back from the others. "Who is Pebbles?"

"Huh? I better let Daddy answer that for you, Ma. What made you ask me about her here?"

"I just. I keep having this dream of a female, and when we got here, I thought of her name."

"Let me call Dad for you. He can explain."

"No! Don't. He gotta lot of work to do. I heard him tell you that much before we left the house."

"Okay, but don't forget to ask him, Ma."

"I won't, and I'm sure you won't let me." They held hands as they caught up with the others. Coco still texted me, letting me know Dija got there on her own and that she had something to talk to me about when I got home.

twenty

TIME FOR CHANGE

ULINDA SAT WITH TILT in the dealership. He had his eye on a used 2009 Austin Martin, white and midnight blue. Since his only job was the inner-city Southside streets, he needed her to drive it off the lot. Ulinda worked for Fox 6 News. Tilt didn't know or care what she did there, just that it paid her well.

"You amaze me, Tilt. Here you go about to spend all this money on a damn car when you don't even have a job."

"Please don't start with that shit up in here. I don't want to hear it. U, you act like I just fuck off my money all the time, when this is the first thing, I've bought for myself outside of a fit here and there in months."

The salesman returned with the paperwork. "Okay, Ms. Telly, I'm going to need your signature here and here—" he pointed "—so I can get you two on your way," he said, handing her the documents.

"Wait, before you sign that." Tilt stopped her. "Man, you sure you can't go lower than this since we buyin' it flat out?"

"I didn't know you were paying cash. Let me call my manager and see what I can do." After a few short minutes with his boss, he said, "How about this, he has okayed me to give it to you for $50K, which includes tax and title and a ninety-day free gas card. What do you say to that?"

"Sounds like a plan to me." Tilt shook his hand, and Ulinda signed off on the car.

"Now why don't you want to drive this car home?" Ulinda spoke into her Bluetooth as she pulled the beautiful car out of the dealership into traffic.

"You know if these folks out here see me drivin' that, they going to swear I stole it an call them boys on my black ass. You're a female, plus you look like one of them. So they won't trip on you," he explained, smoking the last of his blunt as he followed her. Ulinda had pale skin, light brown hair, and green eyes. She was medium built, 160 lbs., and stood five foot nine inches tall. "I can't believe you spent fifty thousand all at once on this car."

"It will be almost a hundred bandz when I'm done with it."

"I bet I don't get to drive it then, will I?" she asked, changing lanes.

"Why wouldn't you? You know you, my bitch. That's why I trust you the way I do. I don't fuck with nobody else like I do you."

"I know, bae. You tell me that all the time, but you won't move in with me. I don't understand that. Why is that so hard for you to do, Tilt?"

"Oh, here we go!"

"Forget it. I'm not going to start on you. Just come over and give me what I need tonight before you go out with your boys."

"Before and after?"

"Yeah, I did this for you, so now you got to do me." She was smiling, looking over at him driving her Land Rover next to her. "I can do that, but I don't know why you think I'm goin' out with my niggas."

"Because you are."

"See, that's where you wrong at. I got two tickets to Mike Epps, and I don't plan going with no hard leg when I got all this butt, I mean beauty, in the car next to me."

"You taking me for real? Don't play. We never go to places like that together," she explained excitedly.

"I'm not playin'. As a matter of fact, I got to make a few runs. Take that car on Fourteenth an North and drop it off so they can get it right for me. My Chevy there, so you got a way home. On your way, stop in the hood so I can give you this money for your hair and our outfits. You know my swag, don't be funny."

After a few more words, he got off the phone with her and called Kill Rob. "Wuddup, fool?" Killa answered.

"Shit, where you at? I need to ride down on you."

"I'm floatin' in traffic, but you can catch up with me at Midtown. I'm about to be there in a second so this girl can get her some ice cream."

Tilt heard Killa Rob's baby mama's voice in the background. "Tell her I said wuddup and give me a few. I'm on Brown Deer."

"It's good. We're gonna be here for a while, but don't be all day. I got some easy money online for us if you want to get it."

"Always with that. See ya in a few." Tilt ended the call, turned up Big Sean, and then put the peddle to the floor on his way to the Midtown shopping center.

~ ~ ~

I missed Duda even though we talked almost daily. I understood his position with the care of his wife and family. Yes, I wanted him, but I want him happy more. I picked up a few extra hours at my job at Deerwood Senior Residences to keep busy. His wife had picked a great time to come back from the missing.

"What time do you get off work?" Mist asked while applying her eyelashes.

"Any minute now. I'm waiting on Betty to get here to relived me. Why you ask? What you got up?" I broke a piece of the Star Crunch cake I was eating and popped it in my mouth.

"Shit, girl, I'm just asking. I'm getting ready for work myself. I really don't feel like this shit tonight, but it's easy money, an I got to get it."

"Have you ever thought about having your own business? Being your own boss for real?"

"What do you got in mind, because I can tell from the way you said it that you've been thinking about it."

"Something like a senior center or a senior house." I sipped my grape soda.

"I don't know a damn thang about taking care of no old folks, unless you want me to give them lap dance and teach the women how to give 'em." She laughed so hard she dropped the phone.

"Girl, you can do more than that. The classes aren't hard, and most of them you are during the day, so you don't get to miss working at that nasty-ass club."

"I never told you this, but I didn't finish school. I don't even got my GED."

"They will help you with that, and I will help. I seen something around here. I'm going to look for it and bring it to you."

"You serious about this, ain't you?"

"Dead serious now that we talking about it."

"Well, okay, I'll do it. Hell, I can't think of nothing better to invest my money in. Spend money to make money, right?"

After a few minutes, Betty showed up for her shift, and I got off the phone with Mist, so Betty's punk ass wouldn't have shit to tell on me. Her ass was over forty-five minutes late. I didn't care as long as they stayed out my way.

In my car I was thinking of my talk with Mist. I decided to call Duda and ask him would he help me by leasing me one of his houses or selling it to me so I could do what I liked with it. I tried him twice, and he didn't answer. I knew he must've been busy and would call me back, so I didn't leave a message.

~ ~ ~

"When my nigga get here, I gotta holla at him at him about some shit. I won't be long. Is that alright with you?" Killa Rob asked Treissa.

"Why you asking me now when you already told him to meet you? I don't see the choice I have."

"You right, I did just tell Tilt that, but it's always the choice of you gettin' yo' smart-mouth ass the fuck out and walkin'." He playfully pulled the truck over.

"Don't play with me, Robert, before I got to show you who the real killer is in this bitch." She made a gun with her fingers.

They pulled in and parked right in front of Culver's so his truck could be found easily. Then he and Treissa went inside and found an empty window seat where a bouncy waitress took their orders. "How come we can't ever have a day to ourselves? We always gotta do this and that, or one of your niggas is up with us."

"I'm the nigga you chose to be with. You knew what I was about befo' you made up your mind to give me yo' number four years ago. Ma, I understand now that you are about to have my son."

"Daughter."

"Son! You want me to get outta these streets. If all go as planned, that's what I'm gonna do. But if I do this for you and get out the game, you gotta do me the honor of being my wife."

"Did you just ask me to marry you?"

"Is that what you heard?"

"I don't see no ring nowhere, so I must've heard you wrong." She looked at the growing line of cars outside. "You know you can't play me for your fool, Robert. I love you, and I want to spend the rest of my life with you, but try to run, run." The four-an-a-half-karat ring cut her words short. Tears of joy fell from her eyes.

"What were you sayin'? I was going to wait until later, but I've made you wait long enough. So, are you or not?"

"Yes! Yes, you know I will!"

twenty-one

THIS WHO

I WAS PULLING INTO my parking space when my cell rang back Duda's tone. "Hello, were you busy?" I answered, stepping from the car.

"Hello. This, this isn't Marqsheo. He's in the shower."

"Then who is this?" I already had an idea who it was; I just couldn't believe she was calling me.

"Khadija. His wife, I guess." She sounded unsure of what to say. "I was just calling you back to ask if we could meet and talk. Marqsheo told me who you are to him and."

"So, what do you want to talk about if he told you? I'm pretty sure he didn't lie to you, so what do you gotta say to me?"

"It's nothing to get upset about. Maybe I shouldn't have called. I'm sorry! I'll tell him to call you when he gets out of the."

"Wait! We can talk. It's just odd to have you call me, that's all." I was now in the house stripping off my work clothes in the bedroom.

"Is it okay if we talk in person?"

"That's cool. Where you want to meet?" I wondered what she could want with me. Duda told me he told her we were friends. Maybe she wasn't buying it anymore.

"I don't know. My memory ain't that good these days." She let out a little laugh.

"Do you know how to get to Applebee's downtown?"

"It's in the mall, right?"

"That's it. Can we meet in an hour? I'm just getting in from work?"

"That's fine. I'm buying since I got you away from what you were doing to meet with me."

"Okay, I'll see you in an hour." When she ended the call, I didn't know what to think. I knew I was going to put on my A game. I had to look my very best for the meeting. I thought of calling Duda back and telling him about the call from his wife. I dismissed the thought, telling myself this would be woman to woman, and wrapped my hair before I stepped into the shower.

~ ~ ~

"U, I know you've put up with my shit for a long time now. I feel I owe you so much. I ain't never told you this shit before because I was too worried about ya not respecting my gangsta. But fuck that shit. All I care about now is having you. I didn't know where I was going or truly who I was before you. Ulinda, you give me purpose in the world where before I had none. So, with this ring and before God, I'm asking you, will you marry me?"

"Oh my God! Oh my God!" she cried, hugging me so tight I thought I was gonna have to knock her upside her head to get her to let me go. But she said yes. And made this gangsta the happiest thug nigga on earth. What? Don't y'all think she deserves for me to put a ring on her finger after sticking with me for three hard years of my bullshit? Hold that thought for a sec. I gotta answer this call. "Hey, Granny, what up?"

"Where are you? You need to come to the house now. Tracy is missing, and the door is broken down on her house. I got the kids, but don't nobody know where she is."

"What! I'm on my way."

"Did I just walk in on what I think I did?" Tilt looked at the ring Killa Rob still held in his hand. "Oh, I get it now. You want me to knock her off for the insurance money after y'all get hitched. I'm with that. I don't like her punk ass anyway. Look at you over there all emotional crying and shit," he teased.

"Tiltton, don't start. I'm not goin' to let you fuck this up for me." She wiped her eyes.

"How many times I got to tell you that's not my name. I'll tell you what, as soon as I have a son, I'ma name him that just for you."

"Bae excuses us, we're gonna step outside to talk. I'll only be a few, promise." Killa Rob slid the ring on her finger before getting out of his seat.

Outside, they sat in Killa Rob's black-on-black Ford F350. "You said somethin' 'bout makin' some money, so what I gotta say can wait." Tilt rolled a blunt. "Since you about to be married man an shit, you light up." He passed it. "What made you ask her to marry you anyway? The baby?"

"That's part of it. She been down for me almost from day one. She was there all the way when I had to do that eighteen-month fed bit for that heat. She didn't even stress me about runnin' the streets when I got home. I only hear it when y'all fools fuck up her time with me."

"I get the same shit from U and Tracy." Tilt took a pull of the good smoke. "They both good to

me, but I don't know if I'm ready to commit yet.
I'm damn sho ain't ready to get outta these streets.
It's what I do. I'm a block bleeder. I need cash
money money to make me retire."

"All that! Well, my nigg, I can't get you that,
but if you bust this move with me, I can get you
Mill in a couple months aside from the $150K you
could just walk away with," Killa Rob casually
tossed his proposal out there, then took a deep pull
off the blunt, studying Tilt's face, waiting for his
response.

"Who do I got to lay down?" He reached for the
blunt. "I'll kill a bitch nigga mama and dog for that
typa bread."

"Do you know who Santos is?"

"No. Should I know the nigga?"

"Man, as long as you been in these streets, you
should. He's a major plug on whatever you need."

"So you want to hit your plug?" This was a
shock to hear to Tilt. He shopped with Killa Rob,
and if he did something like this, who would they
cop from? he wondered.

"We gonna hit him, yeah, but he ain't my plug."

Tilt relaxed.

"We gonna cut his feet out from under him by knockin' his team. Them ATC niggas, Duda and Toochie. Then we move in and take over their spots."

"I'm with that."

"First, I need you to off that nigga Lac bitch ass."

"What that fool Lac gotta do with this?"

"His foul ass made me look bad in front of my people after I told him not to. I would do it myself, but I use to skip school with the punk an' all that. So do you got me?"

"Fuck him! He yo' school-skippin'-ass guy, not mine." Tilt chucked "It'll be handled ASAP. I'm taking U to that show tonight, an after that, I'm on it. I know where to find the nigga."

"Cool. Now what did you want to holla at me about?"

"Ahh, man, I need to get fresh, but it ain't a rush. When you break away from the wifey get up with me."

twenty-two

LOVE OR FEAR?

"IT'S BEEN TWO MUTHAFUCKIN' weeks and you ain't gave me yo' answer to what I asked you yet!" Cadillac snapped at Mist, who'd sat down at his table between her sets at the club.

"What?. Toochie." She had hoped he would just forget about it, but that seemed now to be just wishful thinking.

"Bitch, you know that's what!"

"Well, damn. You don't gotta talk to me like that. I'll do it, daddy, but you better not let it get back on me. I can't afford the bullshit."

"Don't tell me what I better do or not do. It won't get back to you as long as you don't give yo'self away. I know it's been a while since you did this. I'ma make sure you alright," he lied." Now why don't you go get me another drink?" He slapped her on her butt as she walked by him, thinking of how he would make her pay for what she did to him.

~ ~ ~

I watched Khadija nervously take a big drink of her Long Island. "This is nice and strong."

"They make the best Long Islands, if nothing else." I never had drinks with the wife of the man I was seeing. I couldn't help smiling as she licked her full lips. She was much prettier in person. I took a bite of my blue cheese-dipped wings, still suspicious of this meeting. True, her story was unbelievable. Hell, for me to be sitting here with her trying to help her reconnect with the man I loved was truly unbelievable. I knew I should be more concerned about, but it was something about her that I couldn't pull away from. As I listened to her, the fading light from the nearby window framed her face. I felt myself being turned on by her. "You don't remember no part of your marriage? Duda, your kids, nothing?" I was amazed by what she was telling me.

"I have dreams of things all the time. I feel they are more than just dreams, but I don't know which ones to believe. Like you just said, my kids. I don't know nothing about any others, just Coco. But I've had flashes of birthday parties and things like that for others.Two little boys, I think." She took a sip of her second drink before she spoke again. "I know you and Marqsheo were more, and I can see what he sees in you. You're very sexy."

The way she licked the dressing from her lips was almost orgasmic. "Do you remember being with a woman?"

"What do you mean, like in a relationship?"

"Yeah. From what I was told, you and Duda—Marqsheo—and her were very much in love and happy." I had to take a drink after saying that. I didn't want to cause Duda any pain, and now I was thinking I shouldn't have come.

"Pebbles," she said almost to herself.

"Was that her name?" I knew it was. I wanted to see if she did.

"I think so. I'm not sure, but I see this woman's face sometimes when I close my eyes, and the name Pebbles always pops into my mind."

"Have you talked to him about this at all?"

"No, I haven't even slept in the same bed with him since I been there, and he suppose to be my husband." She shook her head.

"Girl, after a few more of these, you will be able to do it all." We laughed. "Do you want to get out of here? My roommate works at a strip club. We can pretty much drink for free there."

"Sure, especially if the girls there look as good as you." She didn't break eye contact with me. It was very clear we were feeling each other. "What about my car?"

"We can take your car there. You just got to follow me to Hillside to drop mine off by my sister's."

She paid the bill, and I gave a tip. On the way to my sister's, I opened my sunroof in hopes that the night air would cool the way the drinks had me feeling.

twenty-three

NIGHTHAWKS

It wasn't until ten o'clock that the strip club's crowd picked up. Wednesday night was amateur night, so the club was filled with a lot of newcomers as well as reggies, as Mist called the customers that regularly came into the establishment. It wasn't long before she spotted her target and his crew of two.

As always, Toochie was dressed to impress. His ice was blinding, and so was that of the men with him. The other seemed to be plainly dressed in a thugged-out way, only showing a modest-looking iced-out watch until he spoke or smiled. All of his bling was in his mouth. Mist could tell that he was the block thug of the bunch. He was Dickie down to the black Air Max 95s on his feet.

"They got our spot open. I don't see our girl nowhere, so we better hurry up before somebody get it," Toochie said.

"She over by the bar."

Lorenzo pointed to Mist, who looked up just in time to see them.

"Who's that? Call shorty over here." Blu showed his blinding smile.

Mist met them at the booth. "I knew you would be your ass in here tonight if I didn't know shit else."

"You act like you missed us or something," Lorenzo said.

"Why do you think this spot was open?" she said, taking the drinks from the waitress. "Their Coronas on me."

"Good looking out. When do you go up?"

"I got about six girls ahead of me after her. What happen to you last weekend? Y'all missed out. It went down in this bitch."

"I was away on business." Toochie pulled her down in his lap.

"Whatever, nigga. You know you had your ass down there at Silk with them stuck-up skinny bitches."

"The only thing we like thin is this ten." Blu pulled two stacks of bills from his pocket. "I'm talking bandz, not dollars." He gave her his smile.

Seeing Mist on the task he put her on, Cadillac and one of his goons went outside to smoke. "Lac, check them hoes out in the Audi over there."

He seen two woman kissing in the front seat. "Maybe we should go see if they need some help with anything," Cadillac joked.

~ ~ ~

After the show, Tilt dropped himself off on Thirty-Seventh and Galena. "You said you were coming to the house tonight. What happen to that?"

"Nothing, U, I'll be there. Me and Tone got to make a run to handle something, and when I'm done, I'm coming straight to the crib. You taking my car, so you know I'll be there."

"If you stand me up, I'm going to peel that little-ass head on your shoulders, then go to work on the one in your pants." Ulinda got out of the car and hugged him.

"I got your fool-ass nigga! Who the fuck is this bitch, Tilt?" Tracy ran up and pushed them apart.

"What? Bitch, don't worry about who the fuck I'm with! Bitch, why you over here?" She tried to hit him in the face, but he caught her hand and shoved her to the ground. "Bitch, don't make me knock you the fuck out!"

"Fuck you, nigga! You ain't shit! I'm gonna call the police on yo punk ass!" Tilt snatched her phone outta her hand. "Give me my phone."

He slammed the cell phone on the ground next to her face. "Bitch, don't ever threaten me!'"

Tracy rolled out of the way and stood up. "You bitch-ass nigga! You gonna get yours."

Tilt started to charge at her, but Tone grabbed him by the arm, stopping him. "Fuck this bitch, fam. We got shit to do."

"U, get in the car and go now! I'll be there when I'm done." He could see that Ulinda was upset, but he knew she would do what he said now and let him have a mouthful later.

"Fam, have her drop Kiwi off fo' me. I'ma go straight back to the trap when we done."

Tracy tried to run to her car so she could follow Ulinda, but Jesse cut her off, kicking her car door back shut. Ulinda hastily pulled off with Kiwi, but not before witnessing Tilt draw his gun and begin firing at Tracy's car. "Bitch, if I ever see you around here or if you come at me again, I'll kill you!" he snapped after shooting out the car's tires.

"I'm sorry! Baby, please don't do this to us! Please?" she distraughtly begged him.

He tossed a few crumpled bills at her. "Get it fixed." He turned to Jesse. "Folks, call Ed to tow this shit away from here, and see if he got some tires," Tilt commanded.

"Why he got to do it? What you 'bout to do? Run behind that white bitch? I don't need him to."

"Shut the fuck up before I change my mind and beat the shit out of you here, bitch!" he snapped. "Let's go, G, before I kill this stupid bitch." Tilt didn't even look over at Tracy again. As nonchalantly as he could make it seem, he dropped into the passenger seat of Tone's car.

~ ~ ~

I didn't want to crowd Khadija. I let her sleep in our bedroom while I slept in the boys' room, so she wouldn't be uncomfortable. Whatever I could do, I did, so when she said she was going out on her own, I agreed with her. What did I know? It might be good for her and to help our family mend its broken pieces back together.

Before I left the house, I set the GPS on her phone. "Call me if you need anything. I set your speed dial, so press any number one through five, and you will reach me or somebody to help you."

"I'll be okay. I'm going downtown. I shouldn't be gone long," she assured, giving me a shy kiss on the lips.

"What was that for?" I asked, surprised because it was her first real attempt at physical contact.

"Do a wife need a reason to kiss her husband?"

"Not at all. It just shook me that all."

"I'm sorry!"

"Don't be. You didn't do anything wrong. I gotta go. I'll see you later. Remember, don't hesitate to call me."

"I won't."

"Your cards are all good if you want to buy somethin'. You can get money off any one of them if you need cash for anything," I yelled back to her on my way out the door.

I made my usual rounds before going into the shop. "How's Dija? Do she remember you yet?" inquired D-Man after handing the pack to one of his runners to take in the spot.

"She good. I don't know what she remembers, but today she went downtown by herself. I don't know why. She been doin' everythang like that with Coco."

"You just let her go?"

"Yeah, she grown. Plus, her phone's GPS is on, so I can track her if I think somethin' wrong."

Right then the police turned onto the block. "Let me get out of here so them fags won't fuck with you. But I gotta holla at you about that nigga Lac when you get some free time."

"Alright, I'll call you when I got time fo' us to get together on that," I promised him before he got out and walked over to where two females stood talking.

I checked the tracking on Khadija's phone as I pulled away from the curb, just to see if she made it downtown. From the map, she was in the mall. A sadness came over me when I thought of how she and Peb use to spend hours at the malls or online shopping. After putting in time at the shop with Arie and Jamarvya getting payroll done and addressing any other issues that needed my attention, I made a few more drops on my way to see Keys and to take my Pops his ham-and-swiss cheese sub he had her text and ask me to bring him.

When I got home, I seen Dija wasn't back yet. "Your mother been home yet?" I asked Coco, who was sitting on the deck with her friends.

"Nope. What time did she leave? We ain't too long got here."

"Don't worry about it. She went downtown; you know how y'all get in them malls." Just then, Toochie's tone played. "Wudd it do?"

"Man, tell me you comin' out tonight. It's gonna be some fresh faces in the club, and you need to get your ass outta that house."

He was right. I did need to let myself be seen, so niggas knew I was still around. "I been out and about all day in my baby. Where you at?"

"I'm on my way from Fond du Lac with Blu. So, you brought the Judge out?"

"What, he pulled out on us?" Blu asked.

"Yeah, the nigga don't fuck with us no mo' an shit."

"Man, it ain't even like that. I'll be there tonight. Tell Blu I heard about the '68 Firebird he caught. Whenever he ready to run it, let me know."

"We can do it whenever. I got a stack on mine."

"Alright, we on this Sunday at the track, and just so you know, I take all major credit cards, too, nigga."

"Alright, alright, how about we all pull out tonight at the club and show them how the big boys do?" Toochie said.

"I'll see y'all there."

I texted Jamarvya and told him we were pulling the old schools out at the club tonight. He texted back and said he would be there in his '77 Monte Carlo. Earlier he told me that he just sat it up on 26s, so I knew he was eager to show off. I sent D-Man the same text since, to say we needed to talk. He had a '69 Dodge Coronet that he loved to show off.

I showered, changed, and gave myself a once-over in the mirror, making sure I was right for the night. "I see you all iced up. Where you going?" Coco asked.

"Out for a bit; I won't be gone long. Don't have none of them nappy-head niggas up in here. I don't know when your mother will be here, so keep your phone by you in case she calls or I do, okay?"

"She still at the mall? What time do the Grand close?"

"I'm not sure." I tracked her. "She still there from what her phone says."

"Daddy, do you do that to me when I be gone?"

"Sometimes, if I'm worried about you," I said honestly. "I'm gone. Call if you need me."

On my way to the club, I called Khadija.

"Hey, wussup!" Her words slurred a little.

"Are you drunk?" I could hear a lot of people in the background.

"I'm good. I'm having fun. You want me to come home or something?"

I started to ask her who she was with. "No, you good, but when you get ready to come home, call me or Coco to come get you. I don't want you driving drunk, okay?"

"Whudeva you say, daddy. Are you going to be there when I get there? I may have a surprise for you."

I heard another female laugh. I wondered who she was with but didn't ask. "Just call me when you on your way, and I'll be on mine." She agreed, and we ended the call. I hit Play on my remote, letting the bass from the four 15s and the sound of Young Money take me away.

I met up with Jamarvya, and we trailed each other not far from Toochie's 1970s forest-green Chevelle; Blu's, gray-and-red '68 Firebird, and Lorenzo's '70 Monte Carlo. I noticed a small crowd of smokers standing here and there in front of the door. I seen Cadillac standing to the far side of the club. A feeling came over me that made me grab my gun. When I got out of the car, I texted Toochie to let him know I was there. Then my curiously got the best of me, so I tracked Dija's phone. At the same time my name was called.

twenty-four

HELL'S GATE OPENS

"GURL, COULD YOU MEET me at the door? I don't know this roughneck lookin' new nigga they got working."

"Okay, just call me when you're here," she responded while putting on her heels.

"I'm here already. Gurl, you'll never guess who I'm with."

"Who? Your boo, Duda?"

"No, his wife. She cool as hell. You'll see. Just meet us at the door." When I got off the phone, Dija leaned over and kissed me. It was a kiss that I accepted and matched her passion. "Wow, what was that about?"

"You're just so sexy I couldn't help myself."

"Let's get to the door so she won't get in trouble waiting on us," was all I could think of to say to that.

While we stood in line at the door, cars started to pull in. Some circled the lot, showing off before they parked. Others rode past slow, looking at us in line.

"Marqsheo and my brother is here," Dija said excitedly.

"Where?" She pointed to cars I'd never seen. "You sure that's him?"

"Yeah, I picked out the rims for that car. I'll know it anywhere. I'll be back. I'm going to tell him we're here together, so he won't be shocked. Maybe we can leave together." She smiled.

Before I could say something, she was on her way over to him. I couldn't help but wonder did she just remember what she just told me, or was it something they just done, since I didn't know the car.

~ ~ ~

I looked up, and Dija was coming my way. "What sis doing here?" Jamarvya inquired. He was just as shocked to see her as I was.

"Shit, I don't know." Out the corner of my eye, I saw a car speeding from the back of the lot. "Look out!" I cried, but my words were drowned out by D-Man's loud pipes and bass from his car as he pulled in an parked between us.

I ran and dove for her. The car flew past so close I could feel the rush of air. We hit the ground hard and rolled. The car screamed to a stop, an the passenger opened fire out the window. Quickly up on my knee, I pulled my gun and then looked down at my wife. Her eyes were closed "Bae? Bae?" I shook her and noticed blood on the side of her face before her eyes opened. She shook her head to focus. I felt my heart beating hard in my chest. "You okay."

"Yeah, my head and elbow hurt, but I'm okay." She rubbed her elbow.

~ ~ ~

Toochie and Blu left Lorenzo getting a lap dance from one of the new girls on their way out to us. "Where you think you going?" Mist asked them as they passed her.

"Oh, we ain't gone yet. Duda outside. We about to meet him and maybe roll up one," Toochie answered, walking out the door.

Just as Mist reached the exit herself, gunfire erupted outside. The girls screamed and ran. She heard the Bouncer yell, "Down! Get down!" but she kept going for the door. Outside, right away she seen Cadillac staggering toward the door of the club. His right side was soaked with blood.

~ ~ ~

I looked for the others. Blu was behind a minivan. He had been shot in the leg. Toochie was next to him between the van and a car.

The car turned around with the shoulder still hanging out the window. I took aim just as a second round of gunfire erupted from the car. Cadillac was hit twice more before he hit the ground. D-Man shot at the passing car. Lorenzo squeezed off three shots from the doorway of the club. The first two went into the nose of the car; the other hit the back door.

The shooter pulled back and yelled, "Go go go!" I stood and emptied my clip into the back of the car. D-Man joined me. Some shots went through the window. The driver shouted in pain and sideswiped a car as he made his getaway. Other shots blew out the rear window, hitting the shooter in the head as the car rounded the corner, getting away.

~ ~ ~

I got up from behind the car I was hiding behind when the shooting started, to look for Duda and Khadija. "You alright?" I heard Mist asking as she ran my way.

"Yeah. Do you see Duda anywhere?"

"He over there by that truck. I think his friend got shot," she said when she caught up to me.

"Think Cadillac got shoot too." She took my hand, and we ran over to where she seen him fall. When we got there, I screamed. His right eye was missing as he stared lifelessly into the night sky.

"Nooo!" Mist cried.

"Come on, we can't help him. Let's see if the others okay." I had to pull her away from his body.

~ ~ ~

After I helped Dija to her feet, I told her to get in the car and go home, then ran over to where Lorenzo was helping Blu stand up. His leg was bleeding bad. He had lost a lot of blood. Toochie had gotten shot too. The bullet went through his forearm. Other than that he was okay. "Where's Ya at?" D-Man asked.

"I don't know. I didn't see him when we started shooting." We took off in different directions to find him.

A few moments later Khadija yelled, "Marqsheo, Marqsheo, over here! Ya got shot. He's shot!" We ran to where she stood with Queen and Mist.

Queen was doing some first aid to keep him breathing. His head and arm were covered in blood. "Somebody call for help," D-Man yelled.

By this time the first of many police cars had pulled into the parking lot. I got Ya's keys and gave mine and my gun to Dija.

"Take my car home. I'm going to get his out of here." For the first time I noticed Queen and her knew each other, but didn't have time to speak on it. I heard Dija tell her to drive her car. Soon everyone was pulling out the lot.

twenty-five

GOT TO HOLD ON

TILT WAS SHOT IN the shoulder. He felt weak
from his blood loss, but he knew he couldn't go to
the hospital or afford to be stopped, with Tone's
dead body lying beside him. So, he willed himself
not to pass out, forcing his heavy eyelids to stay
open. Tilt kept repeating aloud to himself, "Just
make it back to the hood and you'll be good."
Everything around him was an inconsistent blur, on
top of his vision fading in and out, but somehow
still he managed to keep the car on the road.
Miraculously Tilt made it back to the hood. He
flagged down one of his guys, who was posted out
on the block with a few other youngsters.

"Wuddup, G!" an eager-to-please thug named
Lil Ron greeted him as he briskly strolled over to
the car. "Oh shit! Oh shit! What happen to y'all? Oh
shit, folks, is he dead?"

"Some niggas. Some nigg. tried. to rob us, and
we got to blowin'," Tilt lied, still weakly fighting to
hold on to consciousness.

"Aye, y'all! Aye! Folks shot! Get over here and help me!" Lil Ron shouted to the other guys that he was talking with before Tilt pulled up.

"Aye, aye, I need you to go get Tone's car from over on Twenty-First Street," Tilt instructed while allowing Lil Ron to help him out of the car.

"I know, I seen it. What you gonna do with him?"

"I need you to go get a gas can and some gas." He handed him his keys.

"You going to set the car on fire with him in it?" He frowned.

"Look, we don't got time. He dead, and my blood and prints are all over this car. Go get the damn gas! If you want to touch him, you pull him out when you get back," Tilt ordered in a weak, strained voice.

Taking a brief moment to process what he'd been ordered to do, Lil Ron turned to the others that he called over for help and told them to get Tilt inside the house.

"Don't ask me shit. Just get folks in the house and don't say shit to nobody or do shit until I get back. I'll be right back."

Lil Ron sent a text to Jessie as he rushed off to do what he was told. Once he had Tone's car, he noticed that he hadn't gotten a response to his text, so he called Jessie's phone. Jessie answered right away, and Lil Ron explained to him what all had gone down.

Jesse assured Lil Ron that he was on his way, then ended the call and immediately placed a call to Killa Rob.

"Wuddup, Jess?"

"Aye, man, Tilt got burn just now. I'm on my way to the spot on Nineteenth. I need you to meet me."

"Whoa, what the fuck! Is he good?"

"He was hanging in there when I left him, I guess. Tone didn't make it though. How do you want me to handle it?"

"I don't know, my nigga. Do what you feel and let me know what's up. I be down there in the morning."

"Alright, I'll see you then." Jesse ended the call just as he spotted Lil Ron at the gas station. He made a quick U-turn and went back to link up with him. Jessie pulled up behind him and hopped out of his ride. "What you about to do with that?" he questioned, pointing to the gas can he was filling.

"Folks told me to set the car on fire with Tone in it or pull him out if I wanted to. I don't know what to do, but I don't wanna do neither one of 'em. Tone folk's big brother."

"We ain't gonna do that shit! That fool trippin'. Where the car at?"

"Behind the spot."

"We gotta move it. We can't make the spot hot." With that said, they got in their cars and raced off. Once they got to the car, Jesse seen that Tone would have to have a closed casket from the size of the hole in his head. "I'll let you make the call, Ron, but I think we should slide him behind the wheel and burn it instead of having his OG see him like this."

"Man, I can't drive this car with him in it, straight up."

"I got it. Get me a cover out the house to put over this blood." When they got the car far enough away, they wiped it down with gas to remove the prints, then poured the rest over the body and the inside of the car. Then Lil Ron tossed in a lighter.

They ran back to Jesse's car and raced away to get back to the spot. Tilt was passed out in a chair. "How is he?" Lil Ron asked the smoker who was tending to him.

"He's been in and out. He need to get to the hospital right away."

"Alright, I'll take him. Help me get him in the car." Jesse went through his pockets and found his phone to call Ulinda.

~ ~ ~

I walked barefoot from the shower, meeting up with Khadija in the hall. "Just what I need." I took a cup from the tray she was carrying. "You know he don't drink coffee, right?" Fuck, that was a stupid thing to say. I cursed myself in my head, then apologized and said, "I mean, do you remember that he doesn't drink it?"

"Oh, I know, he likes his cappuccino. I remember one of the first times we went out. It was to a Starbucks, and he ordered it. It was kinda like our first argument, too, because he doesn't want to accept that cappuccino is the same as espresso," she explained, smiling at the memory.

"Did someone tell you that, or did you just remember it on your own?"

"Nobody told me. It just popped in my head just now when you asked that," she explained, walking into the living room. The early-morning sunlight began to pour in through the windows, shadowing Marqsheo as he stood lost in thought with his hands in his pockets.

~ ~ ~

My mind was on the shootout we were just in and my family and friends laid up in the hospital. I didn't know if the guys who did it were aiming for us, or someone else and we were just in the wrong place at that time.

"Marqsheo, here, drink this." Dija handed me a cup.

"And go take them nasty bloody clothes off," Queen said, walking up next to her.

"I was waiting on one of you to get out the shower so I can get in," I explained, accepting the cup and walking into the master bedroom with the two of them in tow. "You never told me, how do you two know each other, or how did y'all know that I would be there tonight?"

"Don't be mad at me, bae. I just needed someone to talk to other than our child. So when she called your phone, I called her back and asked her to meet up with me."

"One drink led to another, and I asked her out to the club. We didn't know you were there until just before hell broke out," Queen explained, staring at my broad chest and shoulders. The lust to hold me to make love to me returned, reminding her of how much she missed my touch. I couldn't read Khadija's facial expression because she suddenly went blank, then started gathering my bloody clothes and putting them in the plastic trash bag with theirs. I didn't know what to do, so I just went with the moment.

twenty-six

NEW BEGINNINGS

SEEING DUDA STANDING THERE naked before
he stepped inside the shower must have sparked
something in Khadija from the way she froze and
stared at his silhouette. "Khadija? Are you alright?"
I asked in a low voice trying not to alarm either
of them.

"I will be," she retorted, then took my hand,
pulled me to her, and pressed her lips against mine.
When I didn't pull away from her, she stuck her
tongue in my mouth, deepening the kiss. I returned
it as we peeled off one another's T-shirts before
stepping in the shower with Duda.

Seeing the shock in his eyes from seeing us step
in there with him together made his manhood rise
instantly. Before he could speak, I covered his lip
with mine, then Khadija joined in kissing both of
us. Soon Khadija and I were both humping our hot,
swelling warmth against his legs while holding him
locked in a passionate three-way kiss. I reached
down and began jacking Duda's hardness. Moments
later Khadija got the same idea and reached down

her husband's sexy body, finding my hand already where she wanted hers to be. Not wanting to be rude, I tried to move my hand, but she grabbed my wrist, holding my hand there until she was sure I wouldn't pull away. When I resumed jacking him, she reached between us and placed her hand on my hot mound. A light shiver shot through me before she began more aggressively moving her fingers in and out of me. I stuck my tongue down her throat as she made me cum.

Duda put his arms around our shoulders and played with our breasts while the both of us continued to fondle his length and balls. Then Khadija pulled away from our lips and slowly made her way down my neck to my breast, licking and sucking my nipples and then his nipples and chest before continuing south. Once squatted between us, Khadija turned her attention to her husband's thick, stiff length.

A lustful moan escaped my lips as she switched from sucking him while wiggling two of her fingers in and out of my wetness to sucking and licking my clit while continuing to caress his balls. Duda broke our kiss, and I looked down just in time to see his nut erupt from him, covering her lips and chin. I pulled Khadija to her feet and got myself a taste of his juice off her lips before dropping down and taking his limp manhood in my mouth. I sucked it back hard, and Duda immediately pulled us from the shower, taking our show to the bedroom, where he put it on us both, fucking us the way we needed to be fucked to solidify our union.

~ ~ ~

Queen pulled my wife to her, kissing her, tasting me on her lips before she dropped down and took her place sucking me. She took my tip into her mouth, sucking as she twirled her tongue around it. I closed my eyes, loving the feeling of the sensation of my blood rushing back to my semihard shaft as Queen brought it back to its full, thick length. She took as much of me into her mouth as she could. I could feel my tip tapping against the back of her throat every time her head bobbed back and forth faster and faster. Dija moaned and bit down on my bottom lip as Queen simultaneously dipped her long fingers in and out of Khadija's hot wetness. I had to stop her before she made me blast off again, so I pulled her up and suggested that we take things to the bed.

The three of us made our way into the bedroom, still dripping wet from the shower. At the bed we stood feverishly kissing and touching. I broke away from their lips and kissed my way down Queen's body, thinking that it was only right to start with her since I had stopped her fun. I dipped my tongue into her belly button, teasing her before heading on south to her garden, but when I pushed Queen down on the bed so I could taste her, Dija pushed me out of the way.

"I need to feel this in me now," she said, holding my hardness in her soft hand, "and I wanna tease you with my tongue," she told Queen, who instantly leaned back, spreading so Khadija could get a good look at what she wanted to enjoy.

"Anything you want," I told her without breaking our eye contact. I started kissing her again as I rolled her tight nipples between my thumbs and forefingers. Queen let out a soft moan, getting more turned on by watching us. At the sound of Queen's lust, Dija turned away from me, bending right over in between Queen's legs with her nice ass pointed toward me. I took a few to watch her rub and suck on Queen's inner thighs before tracing her lower lips with her long tongue.

When she parted them and sucked Queen's clit while she pushed her two fingers into her hole, I took my position. I dragged the head of my hardness up and down between the lips of her wet wet a few times before guiding it into her hold. Khadija went to work on Queen while I pounded in and out of her nice and strong. Soon I felt her body quake as she released waves of her hot cream. Beneath her Queen was doing the same. I pulled out of her dripping box, spun Dija around, and pushed her down on the bed, immediately climbing between her legs. I covered her lips with mine, kissing her deeply as she raised her hips, trying to get more of my thickness in her, but I held back. I only moved the head in and out, loving the way her eyes rolled from the pleasure and need of it. When she got tired of my teasing, she wrapped her legs around my ass and pulled me all the way inside. I fucked her slowly at first, but then increased my pace, and Khadija matched my strokes stroke for stroke the way she always had.

"Oooh, God, I'm cumming again!" she panted after a minute. I was on the edge but not there yet, so I rolled her over, and she eagerly got on her knees. Back behind her, I brought my throbbing hardness to her garden and went for the gold. Queen got into the bed, and Dija began to eat her out as I continued pounding her from behind. I moved to pull out, but she reached back and stopped me. "No, babe, no, fill me with your nut!" she commanded me, and like that, we came together.

Spent, I rolled away, and they easily slid into the sixty-nine position. I sat on the opposite side of the bed and watched the show. Seeing the beauties pleasing each other just inches away, it wasn't long before my length started to stand up again. Both women came and then thanked one another with kisses. After a brief rest, Queen crawled over to me and took my semihard shaft in her hand, and she licked and sucked on it until I was on brick again. Then she lay back down on the bed and spread her legs to me. I slid inside her and went to trying to fuck her silly. Queen pushed me away and turned over.

"I want it in my butt," she panted. Before I could make a move, Dija crawled over to help. She dipped her finger into her own wetness, getting it nice and cum coated, then slid it into Queen's ass.

Queen moaned from the pleasure, and Dija removed her finger, taking hold of my hardness and guiding me into the tight hole. I eased into Queen's ass. Soon I was sawing away in her, making her scream and moan as I did my job. When I groaned and said that I was gonna cum, Queen pulled away and turned over, grabbed my shaft, and let it shoot all over her belly and breasts.

"I'm not making this bed again," Khadija suddenly blurted out, and we all lay there laughing and giggling in each other's arms.

twenty-seven

VISITING TIME

KILLA ROB WENT TO the hospital to see Tilt
early that morning. "How you feeling, my nigga?"

"It hurts to breathe at times, but I'm good. They
say they just wanna keep me for a few days to see
how my lung holds up," Tilt explained, giving Killa
Rob's fist a pound. "Wuddup, though, I know you
ain't just come to visit?"

"I didn't want to talk over that hot line is why I
came. Fam, you got your man and brought it to
them ATC niggas at the same time. It's a few of
'em here, so I'ma leave somebody here with you
just in case them fools put two and two together and
come for you."

"Alright, my nigga. Leave me a burner too. I
feel naked without one."

"Man, them people might come see you about
yo gunshot, and I don't want 'em to catch yo with
it. If it would make you feel better, I'll put two
muthafuckas in here with you."

Just then Ulinda walked in. "Hey, bae, I got here
as soon as I got the message. I would've been here

sooner, but after that shit with that bitch, I drunk myself to sleep. I'm sorry! What happened? Are you okay?"

"U, give us a second, ma, alright?"

"Okay." She turned to walk out of the room.

"You don't got to go nowhere." Tilt stopped her. "Fam, I want Jesse up here with me, and I want you to put Lil Ron with Tracy crazy ass. She tell everybody she my bitch, so who knows who knows where she lives?"

"What about U?"

"She good. Don't nobody know where she at. Unless you want somebody with you?" Tilt asked, looking her way.

"Whatever you feel is best, bae. I'm good with it. I took a few days off work, so I'll be here with you." She took the tray of food from the nurse and set it up for him.

"Lil Ron in the waiting room. Him and Juice been here with you all night. I'm sending him on his way to Tee house, but I need Jesse, so Juice got to stay here until we done."

"Fam, folks good. Send Lil Ron in here before you go. I need to see if he handled that last night."

"I'll send him, but he got it done." With that, Killa Rob was gone.

~ ~ ~

"Girl, that's fucked up niggas shot up the Border last night," Keys said, lighting up her blunt.

"I'm glad bro bro alright. Tee Tee said she think her baby daddy Tilt had something to do with it. Because he all of a sudden got shot up last night, too, and he got a nigga at the house with her and the kids." Shonda pulled in the parking spot in back of the apartment.

"Here, I'll be right back out. I just got to grab this work for John John and see if Pops need something while we out." As soon as she was in the building, she called me. Her call woke me up to find I wasn't just dreaming but in bed with Dija and Queen. Keys told me what she heard, and I got right on it. "Speak to me, fool."

"I got word who was behind that shit last night. I need you to put somebody on seeing what hospital the nigga Tilt in."

"Say no more; I'm on it. I'll hit you when I got it." D-Man said, banding up stacks of cash from the night and morning run.

"If you need me, I'll be at the hospital visiting Ya with Dija, room 236."

"Alright, my nigga. Oh, you know Blu got jammed last night on a DWI?"

"Shit, that's fucked up to be shot and in jail. Did anybody go get him?"

"Can't, the fool gotta punk-ass PO hold, so he got to wait on that to come off."

"I'll have Tywannie call his PO to see what she could do. I'll keep you posted."

"Alright, my nigga."

~ ~ ~

D-Man entered the hospital through the back way. He was a little surprised to see Queen sitting outside of Jamarvya's room. "Why you out here?"

"I felt a little out of place; it's all family in there."

"Shit, you better get use to it because you just as much as family now."

"I guess you're right," she answered, thinking about last night.

They knocked and walked in together. "Wuddup, Ya, it's good to see you still here."

"I'm tougher than I look, and I don't plan on checkin' out for a long time," he said, giving D-Man their signature handshakes.

"Duda, let me holla at you out in the hallway right quick." We walked out the room. "Tilt is here in room 214 around the corner from here. I already walked past and seen his name on the clipboard outside the door."

"Let's go see what's on the nigga's mind then. I'm curious to know who he was gunnin' fo'."

"I know you would say that. Here I know you don't got yours on you."

"You got it all planned out I see. Let me tell Ya what's up and the girls. I'll be right back." I put the gun on my waist and the extra clip in my back pocket before going back into the room.

twenty-eight

NO TALKING

JUICE, ULINDA, AND TILT sat listening to Lil
Ron as he told them how things went down last
night. "Man, fam, I pulled you out the car just in
time before it blew up." This was his way of telling
Tilt he had carried out his orders to the letter. "Hype
buddy Omar helped slow up your bleeding until we
got you to the hospital."

"Make sure you remind me to look for him."

"I already hit him with a couple of grams and
some cash. That Killa told me to do for him."

"Okay, now as I said, remind me to look out for
him. Doc said if it wasn't for him stuffing the
wound, I wouldn't be here. So, I got to hit his hand
for doing what he did."

"I feel you," Lil Ron responded.

Nobody really knew what hospital Tilt was in,
and the few that did know knew to call up before
they came. The nursing staff was even told to be
sure to knock before entering. So when Juice heard
the soft click of the door handle being turned
slowly, he sat up. Seeing the gun first and would-be

assassin second made him yell for Tilt to look out while getting out of the line of fire himself. Tilt dropped off the side of the bed just as shots whizzed past, hitting the pillow and the window behind him, sending a shower of glass down on the people below.

Lil Ron pulled his gun from his waist and pushed Ulinda into the bathroom. "Stay down!" he ordered. Ulinda's eyes showed her fear as she lay flat on the cold floor.

Juice traded shot with us through the door.

We took up a new position outside the room, waiting for them to come out.

They slowly pulled open the door. "Fam, I'm going to try to make it to the room across the hall so I can see who ate up. You got me?"

"Just make it fast." With that Lil Ron pulled the door all the way open and dashed across the hall. A spray of bullets lined the wall, just missing him. Juice sent shots back down the hall, hitting the first of the two responding police officers who rounded the corner by the nurse station.

Lil Ron waited for us to make our next move. He didn't have to wait long. I leaned from behind the nurses' station firing three rapid shots. My shots

flew by too close for his liking, and he began
to pray.

"Lord, please help me outta this. Please, Lord!"

D-Man timed him, then sent shots into the room,
hitting Juice in the neck and shoulder. Then he
jumped up, running, zigzagging his way down the
hallway as police officers gave chase. I fired in their
direction, making the officers dive into a nearby
room for cover. This bought D-Man some time to
put some distance between himself and the officers.

Lil Ron shot back at me. I ducked just in time,
then took aim, leaning across the top of the counter
and waiting for him to show himself. He hesitated
for a moment, then made a dash back across the
hall. When he did that, I ran in the opposite
direction because things had gotten too messy. I
would just have to get up with these fools at a later
date, I told myself as I sprinted away. I made it
outside, but thats as far as I got.

"Stop! Put down the gun or I'll shoot!" a
trigger-happy cop exclaimed with his gun aimed at
my head.

Seeing no way out, I did as I was told and was
instantly rushed by a team of officers and slammed
to the ground face first, chipping my two front

teeth. They kneeled on my back as they cuffed my hands behind my back. I caught sight of D-Man standing in the growing crowd that formed outside of the hospital watching my arrest. Knowing there was nothing that he could do for me at that time, he reluctantly made his getaway.

~ ~ ~

"What's going on? Why is people shooting at us?" Ulinda whispered, huddled down and frightened with tears streaming down her face.

"Hush, not now. Where's folks?" Lil Ron asked as he checked to see if Juice was alive.

"I. I. I don't know what happen to Tilt. I just opened the door because I heard all of the shooting stop," she replied. Then they heard Tilt kick the closet door with the last of his strength before he fell unconscious. "Helllp! Help us please! We need a doctor in here! Please help them, please!" Ulinda yelled as she rushed out into the hallway looking for assistance.

twenty-nine

NO VACATION

AS SOON AS I was processed through the
Booking Room of the Milwaukee County Jail, I was
held without bail because of out-of-state ties. After
almost sixteen hours, I was moved from the Intake
Department up to housing pod 5-D cell 43. I was
happy to see that I'd been placed in a single cell. I
instantly got to making the bed. By the time I was
done I was being summoned by the pod officer to
the desk. There he told me that I had an attorney
visit.

Out in the hallway, I spotted my lawyer Sean
Anderson, standing outside of one of the conference
rooms texting on his phone. "How you doing,
Marqsheo. Your wife called me, and I got here as
soon as I could."

"Sean, I'm glad to see you," I said, shaking his
hand before taking a seat in the back of the
conference room. "How bad am I lookin' fo' this?"

"I couldn't find out all that much before getting
down here to see, but from what information I was
able to gather on such short notice, I can tell you

that these sons of bitches really want you. Your case has been assigned to Judge Wagner's courtroom, and it looks like Jamison will be the DA handling the case. Right now, from what I know, Jamison's case is weak. There's no one who can say that you were one of the shooters, and we have a nurse who stated that she saw you pick up a gun off the floor after you pulled a cop to safety. The nurse's statement alone makes things look good for us. I was able to get a copy of the hospital's visiting log which shows that you, your wife, and your kid were there visiting your brother-in-law."

"So, with all of that what do you think I'm looking at?" I questioned, getting right to it.

"Humm, maybe simple possession of a firearm, if that. I won't know for sure until I have a sit-down with Jamison."

"So how much time does that carry?"

"Nine months county time max. Marqsheo, you have a pretty good adult record, so I'm going to push for a fine and probation. But I'm sure you know how this judge is, so he may ask for a little jail time out of you."

"If he do, it can't be no mo' than nine months, right?"

"Correct," Anderson confirmed, then started collecting his things to leave.

"Cool cool. Aye, can you do somethin' about my bail?"

"I'll try my best. I'll be back to see you in the morning for court. Take care and don't discuss your case with anyone."

"You don't gotta tell me that. I already know how these rats be jumpin' on cases." With that said we parted ways. I was escorted back to my cell because it was after lockdown.

I'ma fast-forward through all of the bullshit that happened next. About a month later, I was placed in the house of corrections. That punk-ass judge had pulled a tech and sentenced me to nineteen months of jail time and sixteen months of probation with a four-month withheld sentence. The state had video of me with a gun in my hand before I helped the officer but still nothing showing clearly that I fired it. It's all good, I got guys doing unthinkable numbers for shooting cases.

Anyhow, even though Dija and Queen made it to every visiting day, I missed my kids, who weren't allowed in the institution. That's some shit when there was a sixteen-year-old kid in the bunk beside mine for a high-speed joyride. Well, there's no secret that the system is designed to destroy families.

The girls told me that Toochie was taking it easy and allowing Lorenzo and Blu to handle things on the streets on his end. Jamarvya was back to his old self, holding things down for me until I came home. The way that he held things down made me really think on retiring from the game. It was one thing that I learned firsthand while doing my time in them walls is that niggas gossip like females, so when I won my appeal and got my time reduced, I told no one. Yeah, I'll be home in less than a month now. Can't wait.

~ ~ ~

Just as Killa Rob pulled off, two almost identical Dodge minivans pulled up outside of the fenced in basketball courts where a close-scoring game went on between the neighborhoods. D-Man was the first to hop out of one of the vans waving the angry AK-47 from left to right spraying hot slugs up and down the courts. He was immediately followed by three more shooters, two with AKs and one with an M-4. The unsuspecting Garfield and Galena street ballers didn't know what hit them as pandemonium suddenly broke out all around them. People were doing everything from dropping from getting shot to simply slipping and falling as they attempted to run for cover. Mothers threw themselves on top of their children, shielding them from D-Man's vengeful assault.

Jessie was on the side of the courts showing off his cooking skills on the grills before the shooting began. He and two others returned fire after retrieving their weapons from the nearby cars. As they emptied their clips, they did care that their little Glocks were no match for the firepower that was being used against them.

Jessie's car was parked a good ways away from where he was taking cover behind a big tree. Once out of ammo, he decided to make a dash to his car. Jessie ran hard, zigzagging his way over to his car as slugs whizzed by him, one so close that it ripped through the body of his shirt.

When he made it to the car, he snatched the passenger door open and dived inside. Shots exploded through his windshield, forcing him to stay low. Jessie didn't just cower inside the car; he reached into the center console and got a spare clip for his gun and reloaded. All set, he took a peek to place the shooters and saw that two of the men with the big guns were walking across the grass, still spraying at his friends. Thinking fast, he started the car and floored it in their direction, instantly drawing their fire on him. He kept pressing forward because the lives of his kids, family, and friends depended on him stopping the shooters.

Jessie wondered who was so bold to shoot up a crowded park in midafternoon. Then he seen D-Man and couldn't believe his eyes. He didn't waste no time on his shock. He just promptly aimed the car and his gun at him. Before he made it, the rapid machine-gun fire chopped up the charging car blowing its motor.

Soon the police force joined the shootout, and D-Man and his men retreated back to the stolen vans and smashed off. Two squad cars attempted to barricade their escape routes. Mikey was driving one of the vans with both of its sliding doors open.

"Folk, wussup. What do you want me to do?" he asked D-Man.

"What the fuck you think? Keep going, nigga!" Lil Ricky yelled back at him as he and D-Man leaned out of both doors of the van, firing on the police cars.

Just as they wanted, the squad cars pulled off, trying to escape the gunfire coming from the charging minivan. As Lil Ricky passed through the barricade, one of the officers got off a lucky shot that blew out the rear tire of the vehicle, but it didn't stop them. The thug continued to storm down Cherry Street until he lost control and smashed into the side of a parked moving truck, killing himself instantly. Dazed but able to focus, the others jumped out of the wreckage running in opposite directions.

The second van was met by the force of the skillful SWAT unit's sharpshooters, whose shots caused the van to lose control and flip on its side. D-Man didn't slow to see what happened next. Instead, he ran harder down the street. Suddenly a champagne-gold-colored Infinity Q50 slammed to a stop beside him.

"Fam, get in!"

D-Man seen it was his guy Gully and didn't wait to be told again. He jumped in the car and they raced away.

Epilogue

KHADIJA

STANDING IN FRONT OF the bathroom mirror, I watched Queen making up our bed. My mind raced back to the days when that would've been Pebbles's country-thick ass making the bed after Duda went to the shower and I went to get the kids up for school and make us breakfast. I miss her and the way our family was back then. Yeah, some days are still are a puzzle to me, but I've learned to take things one day at a time, so it isn't as hard on me. Plus, Queen is a good lover and friend. I basically moved her in with me. I hope Duda feels the same as I do about her living with us because I really like having her there and love watching her because she never wears anything to bed. Just like right now, seeing her sexy self-naked back there almost makes me drool and want to suck her hard little clit until she's shaking as she gives me a taste of her sweet cum drop. Pebbles use to have me turned on, but I don't remember it feeling like this.

Anyways, no more tears, right? All of the memories that I've lost I hope to recreate with her,

Duda, the kids, my parents, and the whole
ATC family.

QUEEN

IN THE MONTHS DUDA had been away from us,
Khadija and I had come along way. I remember our
first sexual encounter without him. It took place
after our first visit with him. I don't have to tell you
that it was an emotional one for all of us. After the
visit neither one of us wanted to be home alone, so I
decided to spend the night over. When Khadija
swung me by my place to pack myself an overnight
bag, somehow, we got to making out in the car. I
don't know which one of us kissed the other first.
All I remember is once I'd taken her inside the
house, the dress she was wearing instantly came off.
Staring at Khadija standing there stripped
completely naked in front of me turned me on even
more than I was already. When she kissed me again,
she pulled off my clothes, and I got so hot and wet
that I almost passed out. We never made it to my
bedroom. We just fell into the 69 position right
there on the living room floor. We licked and
sucked on each other's wet wet warmth until we
both came, moaning with our mouths pressed
against the hot wet folds of our mounds. I basically

moved into the house with her that day. With me being there all of the time, Khadija, the kids, and I are closer than I could have imagined. I'm not gonna keep runnin' off at the mouth about us, though, so on another note.

Mist got her GED and is now working on getting her CNA degree so she can be a real part of my dream for us. I opened Loving Care Senior Residents with the help of my old boss and Pops, Duda's dad. He allowed us to turn one of his apartment buildings into my dream come true as long as he could move in and I promised him that Keys would always have a job there. I promised him that I got her as long as the two of them can keep their weed smokin' to a minimum. Ha ha, that's like asking a fish not to swim. I know how valuable Keys is to the team, so she's good. Now I don't fully know what Duda's plans are when he comes home from jail, but I hope it's to focus on adding to our family and getting outta the game. Either way, I'm here to stay.

TOOCHIE

GET OUTTA THE GAME? Who, me? I never thought of it fo' real to be real with you but gettin' shot makes a nigga see things in a whole new light.

I mean, like, I got money. I got Ariana, who's down fo' me fo' real fo' real. She's helping me get my shit back together. It's because of her that I should have my kids back home fo' good soon. Duda might be right; retirement may be just what it's time to do. As soon as I get up with them Garfield Street niggas.

KILLA ROB

THEM ATC NIGGAS SOFT! Ain't no way a muthafucka gonna touch me or one of mine and still walk these streets! As soon as this honeymoon's over, I'ma really show muthafuckas why my city is known as Killwaukee. I'm back at them ATC lames heads. My whole team's ready. Folks, Tilt is 100 percent again and doin' what he do on the Southside until I give him the okay to move on 'em. My son Prince was born on our wedding night, 8 lbs., 5 oz. Now I really gotta turn up on these niggas. After we bust this next power move, I'ma be known as king on these streets. So, stay tuned.

JAMARVYA

With the big homie being on lockdown, it was my time to shine. I had to help sis hold things down with the family businesses as well as our street shit.

Gettin' shot only made me stronger. Honestly, I think the bullet in my right leg adds to my swagger. But I can't talk to you muthafuckas right now 'cause I'm in the middle of somethin'.

"Fam, hit that bitch again!" Fame punched Tracy in the jaw. "Bitch I'ma ask yo again, where's yo bitch-ass nigga hiding at?"

"Please don't hit me no more. I don't know. I don't know!" Tracy cried out. "I'm telling you the truth. I ain't seen him since he got out the hospital! "Tracy said through badly swollen lips. Her left eye was closed, and she was bleeding badly from a cut over her eye and busted lips.

"I believe her, fam. We been beatin' on this bitch for almost an hour. She would've told us somethin' to make us stop a long time ago, don't you think?"

"You know what? You got a point." I agreed then pressed my burner to the back of Tracy's head. "Since you don't know shit, you can deliver a message to the fool-ass nigga for me. Say good night, bitch!"

To order books, please fill out the order form below:
To order films please go to www.good2gofilms.com

Name:_____

Address:_____

City:_____ State:_____ Zip Code: _____

Phone:_____

Email:_____

Method of Payment: Check   VISA MASTERCARD

Credit Card#:_ _____

Name as it appears on card: _____

Signature: _____

Item Name	Price	Qty	Amount
48 Hours to Die – Silk White	$14.99		
A Hustler's Dream – Ernest Morris	$14.99		
A Hustler's Dream 2 – Ernest Morris	$14.99		
A Thug's Devotion – J. L. Rose and J. M. McMillon	$14.99		
All Eyes on Tommy Gunz – Warren Holloway	$14.99		
Black Reign – Ernest Morris	$14.99		
Bloody Mayhem Down South – Trayvon Jackson	$14.99		
Bloody Mayhem Down South 2 – Trayvon Jackson	$14.99		
Business Is Business – Silk White	$14.99		
Business Is Business 2 – Silk White	$14.99		
Business Is Business 3 – Silk White	$14.99		
Cash In Cash Out – Assa Raymond Baker	$14.99		
Cash In Cash Out 2 – Assa Raymond Baker	$14.99		
Childhood Sweethearts – Jacob Spears	$14.99		
Childhood Sweethearts 2 – Jacob Spears	$14.99		
Childhood Sweethearts 3 – Jacob Spears	$14.99		
Childhood Sweethearts 4 – Jacob Spears	$14.99		
Connected To The Plug – Dwan Marquis Williams	$14.99		
Connected To The Plug 2 – Dwan Marquis Williams	$14.99		
Connected To The Plug 3 – Dwan Williams	$14.99		
Cost of Betrayal – Warren.C. Holloway	$14.99		
Cost of Betrayal 2 – Warren.C. Holloway	$14.99		
Deadly Reunion – Ernest Morris	$14.99		
Dream's Life – Assa Raymond Baker	$14.99		
Finding Her Love – Warren C. Holloway	$14.99		
Flipping Numbers – Ernest Morris	$14.99		
Flipping Numbers 2 – Ernest Morris	$14.99		

Forbidden Pleasure – Ernest Morris	$14.99		
He Loves Me, He Loves You Not – Mychea	$14.99		
He Loves Me, He Loves You Not 2 – Mychea	$14.99		
He Loves Me, He Loves You Not 3 – Mychea	$14.99		
He Loves Me, He Loves You Not 4 – Mychea	$14.99		
He Loves Me, He Loves You Not 5 – Mychea	$14.99		
Killing Signs – Ernest Morris	$14.99		
Killing Signs 2 – Ernest Morris	$14.99		
Kings of the Block – Dwan Willams	$14.99		
Kings of the Block 2 – Dwan Willams	$14.99		
Lord of My Land – Jay Morrison	$14.99		
Lost and Turned Out – Ernest Morris	$14.99		
Love & Dedication – Warren.C. Holloway	$14.99		
Love Hates Violence – De'Wayne Maris	$14.99		
Love Hates Violence 2 – De'Wayne Maris	$14.99		
Love Hates Violence 3 – De'Wayne Maris	$14.99		
Love Hates Violence 4 – De'Wayne Maris	$14.99		
Married To Da Streets – Silk White	$14.99		
M.E.R.C. – Make Every Rep Count Health and Fitness	$14.99		
Mercenary In Love – J.L. Rose & J.L. Turner	$14.99		
Money Make Me Cum – Ernest Morris	$14.99		
Murder And Deception – Warren C. Holloway	$14.99		
My Besties – Asia Hill	$14.99		
My Besties 2 – Asia Hill	$14.99		
My Besties 3 – Asia Hill	$14.99		
My Besties 4 – Asia Hill	$14.99		
My Boyfriend's Wife – Mychea	$14.99		
My Boyfriend's Wife 2 – Mychea	$14.99		
My Brothers Envy – J. L. Rose	$14.99		
My Brothers Envy 2 – J. L. Rose	$14.99		
Naughty Housewives – Ernest Morris	$14.99		
Naughty Housewives 2 – Ernest Morris	$14.99		
Naughty Housewives 3 – Ernest Morris	$14.99		
Naughty Housewives 4 – Ernest Morris	$14.99		

ENTANGLEMENTS

Never Be The Same – Silk White	$14.99		
Scarred Faces – Assa Raymond Baker	$14.99		
Scarred Knuckles – Assa Raymond Baker	$14.99		
Secrets in the Dark – Ernest Morris	$14.99		
Secrets in the Dark 2 – Ernest Morris	$14.99		
Shades of Revenge – Assa Raymond Baker	$14.99		
Slumped – Jason Brent	$14.99		
Someone's Gonna Get It – Mychea	$14.99		
Stranded – Silk White	$14.99		
Supreme & Justice – Ernest Morris	$14.99		
Supreme & Justice 2 – Ernest Morris	$14.99		
Supreme & Justice 3 – Ernest Morris	$14.99		
Tears of a Hustler – Silk White	$14.99		
Tears of a Hustler 2 – Silk White	$14.99		
Tears of a Hustler 3 – Silk White	$14.99		
Tears of a Hustler 4 – Silk White	$14.99		
Tears of a Hustler 5 – Silk White	$14.99		
Tears of a Hustler 6 – Silk White	$14.99		
The Betrayal Within – Ernest Morris	$14.99		
The Last Love Letter – Warren Holloway	$14.99		
The Last Love Letter 2 – Warren Holloway	$14.99		
The Panty Ripper – Reality Way	$14.99		
The Panty Ripper 3 – Reality Way	$14.99		
The Solution – Jay Morrison	$14.99		
The Teflon Queen – Silk White	$14.99		
The Teflon Queen 2 – Silk White	$14.99		
The Teflon Queen 3 – Silk White	$14.99		
The Teflon Queen 4 – Silk White	$14.99		
The Teflon Queen 5 – Silk White	$14.99		
The Teflon Queen 6 – Silk White	$14.99		
The Vacation – Silk White	$14.99		
The Webpage Murder – Ernest Morris	$14.99		
The Webpage Murder 2 – Ernest Morris	$14.99		
Tied To A Boss – J.L. Rose	$14.99		

Tied To A Boss 2 – J.L. Rose	$14.99		
Tied To A Boss 3 – J.L. Rose	$14.99		
Tied To A Boss 4 – J.L. Rose	$14.99		
Tied To A Boss 5 – J.L. Rose	$14.99		
Time Is Money – Silk White	$14.99		
Tomorrow's Not Promised – Robert Torres	$14.99		
Tomorrow's Not Promised 2 – Robert Torres	$14.99		
Two Mask One Heart – Jacob Spears and Trayvon Jackson	$14.99		
Two Mask One Heart 2 – Jacob Spears and Trayvon Jackson	$14.99		
Two Mask One Heart 3 – Jacob Spears and Trayvon Jackson	$14.99		
When Love Happens – Warren Holloway	$14.99		
Wife – Assa Ray Baker & Raneissa Baker	$14.99		
Wife 2 – Assa Ray Baker & Raneissa Baker	$14.99		
Wrong Place Wrong Time – Silk White	$14.99		
Young Goonz – Reality Way	$14.99		
Subtotal:			
Tax:			
Shipping (Free) U.S. Media Mail:			
Total:			

Make Checks Payable to Good2Go Publishing, 7311 W Glass Lane, Laveen, AZ 85339